STRANDED

SHADOWS OF THE VOID BOOK 2

J.J. GREEN

BOOK ORDER

The Books of Shadows of the Void - Complete Series

Prequel: Starbound
Book 1: Generation
Book 2: Stranded
Book 3: Dawn
Book 4: Shadowrise
Book 5: Underworld
Book 6: Burned
Book 7: Trapped
Book 8: Mars Born
Book 9: Shadow Battle
Book 10: Shadow War
Books 1 - 3 The Galathea Chronicles
Books 4 - 7 The Earth Chronicles
Books 8 - 10 The Galactic Chronicles

1

Jas Harrington was watching Haggardy in his cell, looking for signs of alien possession. The man was eating his rations, hunched over a plate as he sat on his bunk, and Jas was looking through one of the clear cubes in the wall, set to observation mode so that he wouldn't know she was there. The former first mate had been in the brig a couple of days, but Jas was no closer to figuring out whether he was infected with an alien, or if he was just the same play-it-safe Haggardy she'd always known and not particularly liked.

When the rest of the *Galathea's* officers had been infected on K. 67092d, Haggardy had been with them, there was no doubt about that. He'd admitted as much himself, but he maintained that he'd managed to avoid the other officers' fate. All that he would say about what had happened was that it had been too dark to see much, and he'd escaped as soon as he could. After that, he'd fooled their dead master, Loba, and the rest of the infected officers by copying whatever they did.

The problem was, Jas wasn't sure what she was looking

for. Possessed individuals looked and behaved nearly the same as usual. Most of the *Galathea's* crew members had been duped by the infected officers, and they'd nearly taken over the ship. Jas had been one of the few to notice a slight change, a certain distant, cold taint to a victim's manner and an emptiness behind the eyes. Her perception was due to her years of working with the part-human, part-synthetic defense units, which had made her sensitive to that touch of inhumanity.

Doctor Sparks had run every test he knew of on the disgraced Haggardy. As far as he could tell, there was no sign of alien infection. The former first mate's DNA, retinal scans, and fingerprints matched those on Haggardy's file. But Jas guessed that the other infected officers would have also passed the tests.

She couldn't understand it. Haggardy's behavior had seemed entirely human ever since he'd been arrested. Before that, he'd gone along with the possessed Loba's plans. Only one thing counted in his favor: when Jas had commanded the defense units to destroy the ship's shuttle so that Loba couldn't take any more of the crew to the planet surface, Haggardy hadn't taken control of the units himself. As the higher-ranking officer, he could have, yet he hadn't. It wasn't enough.

Carl Lingiari appeared at the door to the brig, and Jas's mood lifted at the sight of him. As well as saving all their lives by turning the crash of the *Galathea* into a crash-landing, the lanky pilot had been a helpful support and ally as Jas had organized the crew afterward.

He gestured to her to step outside. "Let's take a walk," he said as they left the brig.

"What do you think about Haggardy?" Carl asked. "Made your mind up yet?"

"I can't make him out," replied Jas. "Whatever he is, he's staying in the brig. He didn't lift a finger to stop Loba and the others. I don't trust him. He's a traitor."

"I hope Polestar agrees. We better have a pretty good excuse for locking up the first mate."

"When they see the security vids, it should be obvious. Whatever. There's not a lot I can do about it."

They toured the ship's corridors, passing small groups of crew members who were making the best repairs they could to damage caused by weapon fire and during the crash. Jas had assigned everyone tasks to keep them occupied and not dwelling on what would happen now that they were stranded on K. 67092d, which was inhabited by hostile aliens.

It was a few moments before either of them spoke, and then they both spoke at once.

"You go first," said Lingiari.

"Have you been on the bridge? Has anything arrived at the comm desk?"

"I've been there all morning. Nothing's come in from Polestar or anyone else. How long has it been?"

"The fight with the officers was three days ago." replied Jas. "If Lee sent a message packet to Earth like I asked her to, I think a reply should've come by now. Do you know how long a response should take to reach us?"

Lingiari grimaced. "If they replied right away, we should have their answer by now. I checked. A couple of days is plenty of time."

"I know the comm desk isn't displaying sent messages, but will it show if we receive a reply?"

"If nothing's broken, I think it should."

"And if something's broken, would we be able to tell?"

"I suppose we might not."

Jas cursed. "So we can't get a message out, and we don't know if Lee sent one because she's in stasis. We might have received a reply, but the comm desk might not be showing us. Or Polestar might not have replied yet."

"You think the company wouldn't reply right away?"

"I don't know, Lingiari. Maybe they would. Or maybe they're still figuring out what to do about us."

The pilot stopped and turned to Jas. "You mean they might not send a rescue ship?"

A group of men and women working on replacing a section of wall nearby paused at Lingiari's words and turned to hear more. Jas grabbed the pilot's arm and pulled him along the corridor to a deserted area, where they couldn't be overheard. "For krat's sake, be careful what you say around the crew. The last thing we want is people thinking we might not be rescued.

"Look, Polestar doesn't exactly have a good track record when it comes to employee welfare, does it? There's a reason we sign away our compensation rights before embarking on a mission. *We* take the risks, Polestar takes most of the profits, and that's just the way they like it.

"We might not have received a reply because they're still weighing up the costs of a rescue against the potential benefits. We're about halfway through the mission, and we're only at break-even point. We've sent them the information on the planets surveyed up till now. Are we worth the cost of diverting a ship to come and pick us up? Or would it be more profitable to send one to cover the planets we didn't reach?"

"But," said Lingiari, frowning, "even if Polestar decides we're expendable, the *Galathea's* worth billions. They aren't going to give up on her that easily."

"We have to think about the information Lee sent, too,"

said Jas, "assuming she sent it before we crashed. She didn't know we would be stranded. She didn't send a Mayday. She would have told them about the hostile aliens, infected officers, and the threat to the ship. With no more information, as far as Polestar knows they could be sending another ship and its crew into a deadly conflict. Even if Lee sent a packet to them, they haven't heard anything since. They don't know why we've gone silent."

"They might not want to risk another ship," said Lingiari.

"Exactly. Polestar isn't a military setup. That's the responsibility of the Global Government, and in a century of deep space exploration, they've never had to deal with hostile intelligent aliens. If Polestar's told them about us, there's no knowing what they'll do. Whatever it is, rescuing us mightn't be the first item on their agenda."

Some moments passed. "So what do we do?" asked Lingiari.

"I don't think we should be relying on anyone to rescue us. The more I think about it, the less likely it seems that's going to happen. If we're going to get off this planet, we're going to have to do it by ourselves."

"I dunno how," said Lingiari. "I won't be able to lift her into orbit, let alone star jump. Both the starjump and RaptorX engines must be gone after that crash-landing, and we're not gonna find any spare parts around here."

"I've told someone to have a look at the engines. Her name's Toirien MacAdam. She's only an engineer-in-training, but I remember the chief engineer saying he was really impressed with her. Said she was a natural with a wrench."

"Yeah, I know her," said Lingiari. "She did some great work with the shuttle."

"I'm hoping she can do something, enough to get us off

this planet anyway." Jas frowned and looked down. "She's all we've got. The rest of them, the chief, first, second, and third engineers, they're all gone."

Lingiari put a hand on Jas's shoulder. "It's not your fault."

She shook her head. "It was my job to protect them. All of them." The pilot went to speak, but Jas cut him off. "I don't know how MacAdam's going to repair the engines, but we've got to help her try. And we can't forget about the threat on board. We don't know if all the infected officers died. You weren't sure exactly how many Loba took with him to the planet. Possessed personnel could be walking among us right now.

"What's more, Haggardy's sitting in the brig, maybe infected by an alien and maybe not, but he's another threat either way. It wouldn't surprise me if some of the crew think *he* should be leading them, not me."

"I'm waiting for the good news."

"Keep waiting."

2

Toirien MacAdam rested her brow against the hatch on the *Galathea's* outer shell. The cool metal soothed her hangover a little, but the effect was quickly lost when she lifted her head to resume her work releasing the bolts. She would've asked Dr. Sparks for a painkiller, but the fussy man would want to know why she needed it, and he would soon see through her lies. Alcohol and all other drugs were strictly forbidden. He would test her blood and report her. Though in their current predicament, Toirien wasn't sure what difference that would make.

Right then, she had enough to contend with. She didn't need to confirm the doctor's prejudice against naturals and add his disapproval to her list of things she already held against herself. She tried releasing the door's fixings with an electric spanner, but when she pressed the trigger, the machine whirred uselessly. Like all the others, the access hatch had been damaged when the *Galathea* had crashed, and wouldn't open. Toirien replaced the electric spanner with a wrench, and hit the handle of the wrench with a mallet until the fixing released a little. Then the spanner did the work of removing it.

Getting drunk had seemed Toirien's best reaction to being stranded on K. 67092d, though long experience had told her that alcoholic oblivion was only a temporary solution. As was her habit, the previous night's Toirien had chosen to ignore the fact, leaving that day's Toirien to suffer the consequences.

Two more fixings to remove, then she might be able to open the hatch. Why the higher-ups wanted to open the *Galathea* to the outside, she didn't know. K. 67092d harbored dangerous aliens, aliens that had infested the rest of the engineers, leaving her the only one with knowledge of the ship's engines. No pressure, though.

Toirien imagined how drunk she would get that night.

Alcohol—easily made aboard ship—wasn't the only substance she could turn to for a little temporary oblivion. Pills to energize, or soothe the emotions, get you all loved up, or expand the consciousness, were also available, if you knew who to ask. Illegal, of course, on Earth as well as the *Galathea,* and the crew had to pass a drug test to be hired.

There were ways around the test, such as by giving the tester a hefty bribe, but Toirien had been clean when she came aboard. She'd stayed clean, too, but since the crash she'd lapsed, given in to temptation, and leapt off the wagon.

Emitting a grunt, she swung the mallet at the wrench handle. The final fixing loosened, and the wrench swung round before falling with a clatter to the floor. Toirien wiped her forehead with the back of her arm. Though her head still ached, the pain seemed to be lessening. It was the manual labor that did it. She'd always enjoyed the simple, honest, plain work of fixing things, tinkering with engines, taking devices apart, and putting them together again to figure out how they worked. Computer systems with their chips and impossibly fine wires puzzled her, but she understood mechanical devices, and there was a satisfaction to working with them that she'd experienced with nothing else in her life so far. In all other things, she freely admitted to herself, she was a screw-up.

That was it. The final fixing was out, and it was time to test whether the hatch would open. But Harrington, the chief security officer, who seemed to be the one in charge for the moment, had told her not to attempt opening it alone. She'd been instructed to inform the woman when she was ready, and with the comm system out, that meant going to the bridge.

Toirien dragged her bag of tools to one side and set off across the ship.

The beating the *Galathea* had taken as she'd slid across the rocky, barren surface of K. 67092d showed its effects in the walls, floors and ceilings of the ship's corridors. Surfaces were warped, and in some areas they'd split open, revealing the ship's thick metal beams.

The effects on the crew were more subtle, but now that the initial shock of the crash was wearing off, they were beginning to show. Toirien had seen many of her shipmates weeping uncontrollably, while some stared endlessly into space, apparently immobilized by the situation. Others shouted angrily to whoever would listen about the incompetency of the officers who had led them into the crisis.

She arrived at the bridge. A piece of metal had been forced into the door to hold it open. Inside, the red emergency lighting revealed two figures: the chief security officer and the pilot. They were talking, and Toirien hesitated at the door. Authority figures made her freeze up. Too many bad memories. The pilot, Lingiari, spotted her and waved her in.

Toirien hadn't had much to do with either of these individuals previously. Her job had been mostly below decks, servicing and testing the starjump and RaptorX engines. But she knew Harrington by sight. She was a giant of a woman, and with her deep olive skin and striking, dark reddish-brown hair and eyes, she was difficult to miss. The pilot wasn't much shorter than the security officer, and he was well known and liked for his easy smile and his stowaway pet, who had made most of the crew's acquaintance even though he wasn't supposed to exist.

"You've found a hatch you think will open?" asked Harrington. She and the pilot were sitting at the flight controls. The screens were dark.

"I did. I released everything that's securing it to the ship," Toirien replied. "I left it closed, like you said, but it should open with a bit of work, one way or another. That area of the ship doesn't seem too badly damaged, and I don't think there's much force holding it in place. But once it's open, we won't be able to shut it again in a hurry. I'd have to reseal it bolt by bolt."

"Okay, I understand," said Harrington. "What else can you tell us? Have you completed a full inspection of the engines?"

Toirien's brows knitted together. Who did this woman think she was talking to? She was only an engineer-in-training, barely a step above a mechanic. She ran a hand through her ginger curls. "I spent most of today working on the hatch after I got your order. I haven't had time to...I mean, with the crash and everything..."

Harrington didn't try to disguise her look of disappointment. She stood. "MacAdam, you're the best we've got. We're relying on you for our chance of getting off this planet. You understand that, right?"

Toirien shrugged. "I suppose." Seeing Harrington's dark eyes narrow, she added, "I understand."

"Good." The security officer turned to Lingiari. "Shall we get it over with?"

"We're ready as we'll ever be."

"Come with us, MacAdam. We're going to open that hatch."

Toirien wasn't sure she wanted to find out what was outside the *Galathea*. She'd heard the various rumors and the official version given out by Harrington, that the aliens were living inside strange structures on the planet. But what if some of them had scaled the ship and were waiting for them to stick their heads out?

She followed Harrington and Lingiari as they went to retrieve four defense units from storage. At first she thought they wanted the units to help open the door. She didn't think they would be necessary, but she didn't have the confidence to tell Harrington that.

Where they went next, however, made her realize why they needed the units. In an emptied-out cabin was a stack of long, plastic, body-shaped sacks. It was impossible not to understand what was inside. It was the dead bodies of the officers who had been infected by aliens. Somewhere in that pile were men and women she'd worked with, eaten with, joked with.

"What're you going to do with them?" Toirien asked as the defense units shouldered two bodies each.

"We have to put them out through the hatch," Harrington replied.

"You're going to just throw them off the ship?" Toirien blurted.

The security officer's expression was stony. "We don't have a choice. As far as we know, the aliens that infested them are still inside. They could be alive, despite their hosts dying. Even if we had the facilities and energy for storing them, they could infect more crew members. We have to get rid of the bodies, and we don't have any other way of disposing of them. No furnaces or disintegration units on the ship are big enough."

"So you're going to dump them outside, without a ceremony, with no one saying a word over them?"

Lingiari said, "She's right, Harrington. Someone should say something."

"I can't risk anyone getting close to them. It's risky enough for us to do this. The crew can say something later if they want. I don't want anyone hanging around that hatch."

It took the defense units three trips to carry all the bodies to the access hatch. When they'd brought the last one, Harrington asked the defense units to scan the exterior for life forms. They found nothing, so Toirien started work on the final stage of opening the hatch. She gave Harrington and Lingiari crowbars, and together they worked at the hatch, gradually loosening it until it swung to one side, hitting the wall with a resounding bang. After days of emergency lighting, the daylight that flooded in was painfully bright, and it was some time before, blinking in the bitterly cold air, Toirien could focus on the terrain outside.

Harrington had commanded the defense units to be ready with their weapons, but nothing was waiting to attack or force its way aboard. The view of the barren scrubland looked depressingly similar to Toirien's native Ireland. The only relief in the monotonous landscape was a building of dark gray, hexagonal blocks on the horizon.

Lifting and dropping the bodies like sacks of rice, the

defense units did their job. The distance from the hatch to the planet surface was so great, there was no sound of them hitting the ground. Toirien didn't know which of the sacks contained the chief, second and third engineer, and she didn't want to know.

When all the bodies had been disposed of, a unit climbed down the side of the ship. After it had reached the bottom, the bright glow of its flamethrower could be seen as it gave the dead officers an informal cremation. No one spoke. Toirien replaced the hatch's fixings after the unit returned, and the security officer and pilot left.

That night, someone among the crew conducted a quickly put-together ceremony in the canteen to commemorate the lives of those who had died. Toirien didn't remember too clearly who it was that spoke. By the time the ceremony had started, she was already drunk.

3

P ausing on the ladder down to the maintenance tunnels of the *Galathea's* engine, Toirien adjusted her equipment bag over her shoulder. She was going to test the functioning of each section of both engines. The ship's computer was giving confusing readings, so she had to test the sections individually. The process would take her at least her entire shift.

Not that the crew worked in shifts any more. Everyone had been allotted tasks, and they were expected to do them whenever they weren't sleeping or eating. They had to assist with health care, repair, and distributing supplies. It had given them all something to do, but it didn't prevent discussion on how long they would be there, what was going to happen to them, and if they could expect a rescue ship. No one was answering their questions, and the uncertainty bothered a lot of people. It worried Toirien. She knew of crew members who would take advantage of the general feeling of dissatisfaction and despair.

Still, she didn't know what she could do about any of it. She continued down the ladder, the rhythm of her hands and feet matching the pounding in her head from the previous night's binge. Starting at the lowest level, she would work her way up, checking each section methodically for damage. She recalled the violent juddering of the crash. When she thought of what she might find down there, she was overcome with dread. She realized it was that dread and fear that had put her off going into the engines all that time. If they were trashed, and if no rescue was coming from Earth...she swallowed.

Toirien looked up to see how far she'd come. Looking down made her dizzy. The engine access point was a small square high above, brighter than the surrounding lights. She must be nearly at the bottom. As she risked a peek downward, she drew in a breath. The engine floor was directly below, and it was severely warped. The *Galathea* might no longer be airtight, let alone contain working engines. With RaptorXs running, they might have limped to a planet capable of supporting human life, if one were close by. But from the look of the damage, it would be a miracle if anything was working. The engines would need extensive repair and replacement parts. Parts they didn't have.

After a long moment surveying the wrecked floor, Toirien climbed down the final meters of ladder. She stepped into a service tunnel and went to the end, where an instrument panel was embedded in the wall. She had many hours of testing ahead.

~

A LONG WHILE LATER, halfway through her engine check, Toirien took a rest. The testing wasn't going well. Not every panel was giving results. The crash-landing had damaged them, and because they weren't working, she had no way of telling if that section was functioning as it should, except for opening it up and taking a look. Only Toirien didn't know what she was looking for. She hadn't got that far in her training.

She sat on the metal mesh floor and took her lunch out of her bag. She needed a drink, but she'd mustered the self-control to not pack any alcohol. She needed to keep her wits about her if she was going to complete a report for Harrington. It was going to be a short one: without help from Polestar or someone else, they were screwed. She only had to figure out the details of how and why and to what extent they were screwed.

In Toirien's lunch pack, along with her food and water, was something she probably shouldn't have brought with her. She pulled out her personal interface, which contained all the vids, mails, images, and other digitized content dear to her. In the silence and solitude of the tunnel, and after her hours of disappointing work, she couldn't help but open the device, knowing full well that it was a bad idea.

Two faces looked up at her from the screensaver she'd had for years. The sight of the faces tore at the deeply scarred wound she bore inside. They were the faces of two little girls hugging, their curly ginger heads pressed tightly together. They were laughing excitedly. Toirien's thumb swiped them away, only to reveal a more deadly weapon—a list of mails from the girls, which she'd received in the early years when they'd been learning to write, and their memories of her were fresh in their minds.

Mammy, we dont like it here. we mis you. Wen are you comming back? We want to com home. Grace is sad. Pleez com and tak us with you.

I luv you

Joan

Toirien was helpless under the spell of the simple messages. She read each mail, though she'd read them so many times they were etched on her mind. When she'd finished the mails, she watched the few vids she'd made of the girls when they were babies. In some of the vids the camera shook, as if she'd been under the influence of something as she made them. It had taken her a long time to admit it to herself, but she probably had.

She drank in each feature of her daughters' faces. They both closely resembled her. Their ginger hair and brown eyes were the same, and they would probably develop her boxy figure. Some features differed—the looks they'd inherited from their fathers, whoever they might be. Toirien knew it was one of two men who had fathered Joan, but for Grace she had no idea. That period in her life was hazy to her now.

Tears dropped onto the screen, distorting the small, moving images of Grace and Joan playing at a beach somewhere. She wanted to reach through the screen and touch them, grab them, pull them to her, and hold them close, smell their hair, and feel their soft skin.

The device slipped from Toirien's fingers and onto the gridwork floor. She rubbed the heels of her hands into her eyes and smeared her tears over her face. It was her own fault. She'd done it to herself, and to them. She had no one else to blame. The authorities had been right to take Joan and Grace away. Naturally conceived and born to a drug-addicted mother, their future would have been grim if they'd stayed with her. The agency had promised she could have her children back if she cleaned herself up. If she could stay sober and pass all the tests, they could be a family again.

But it had been so hard. Without her children near her,

and suffering the shame of being an unfit mother, and the worse criticism she heaped on herself, she'd found everything harder to resist, not easier. She'd needed to escape then more than ever.

Toirien wondered what Grace and Joan looked like now. Did they even remember her? She rose to her feet, grabbed her bag of equipment from the floor, and threw it against the wall. The tools and instruments spilled out, and the tunnel echoed with their clatter.

Her job, this training, had been the first steady work she'd had in years. It was supposed to have been the start of a new future. A future where she would stay off the booze and drugs, where she would earn enough to rent a small home and prove that she was reliable and fit to be a parent. It was how she would finally get her kids back. But the ship had crashed, and it looked like even if she were as clean as a whistle and the perfect citizen, she would never see her daughters again. They would never know how hard she'd tried, or how sorry she was for what she'd done, or how much she loved them.

4

Opening the doors to the dead officers' cabins was easy. Karrev couldn't understand why more of the crew weren't doing the same and taking whatever was up for grabs. He'd discovered plenty: jewelry, rare perfumes, luxury foods, drink, and other goods from Earth, and expensive alien artifacts. He'd often wondered what it would be like to live on an officer's pay, what they spent their bonuses on, and his curiosity had been more than satisfied with the many items he'd discreetly removed. It wasn't as if the dead officers would be needing them after all, so he didn't see how he was doing anyone any harm. He was just using his smarts. But he'd been stupid, too. He'd been slow to go for the top prize: Loba's quarters.

Karrev pushed open the door, revealing a room that was surprisingly lacking in expensive items, which made the man pause. Had someone got there before him? But the room didn't look as though it had been ransacked.

As master of the *Galathea*, Loba should have had an excess of products to indulge himself with during the long mission. Karrev had never been in a master's cabin before, and he hadn't been sure what to expect, but it wasn't this.

After a few puzzled moments, Karrev shrugged and turned to leave, but something drew him back. The look of the room was oddly familiar. It wasn't austere so much as poor, as if Loba had sold off everything he'd had. As if he'd been short of money, which was crazy, unless...Karrev's eyes widened.

A thrill passed through the man, straightening his stooped posture and brightening his features. He scanned the place, taking in every object, every detail, every potential hiding place. If his guess was correct, he would have to search very, very thoroughly, but it would be worth it. A prize like that would be worth pulling the place to shreds.

Karrev went to Loba's bunk and lifted the mattress. He ran his fingers under the frame. Nothing. Of course not. That was a hiding place for amateurs. It was where the elderly hid their worthless paper money. Neither Loba nor anyone else who could afford his habit was an amateur.

Most addicts needed only a few drops per day. A supply to last a year or longer could be hidden inside a small object.

His pulse racing, Karrev took another look around the room. He would have to be methodical about his search. He would start in one place and work his way out, leaving nothing overlooked. He decided to begin in the deceased master's closet. As he opened the door, his gaze alighted first on a large piece of paper on the floor. Karrev hadn't seen paper for years. He wasn't one to visit art galleries or muse-ums, but he recognized it.

Holding up the sheet, he saw the spread-out figure of a naked man. Lines intersected by points ran from the head and spine to the tips of the fingers and toes. A slow, triumphant smile advanced across Karrev's face. If he'd wanted or needed proof of his suspicion, this drawing was it. He threw the paper down. It was worth a fair bit, but what he was looking for was worth a lot more.

More than two hours later, Karrev sat on the floor in the center of the master's cabin, his brow deeply creased. Around him, the room was in complete disarray. He'd pulled apart and discarded every one of Loba's few possessions. The closet shelves, desk drawers and bunk were empty, and the floor was covered in detritus. Karrev had even dismantled the comm system. Its innards were spread out, smashed in a moment of frustration.

It had to be there somewhere. He reminded himself that he needed to stay calm. He needed to focus on the task. Loba hadn't been stupid. He wouldn't have risked hiding it anywhere else aboard the ship. His cabin was the only place he could have guaranteed his privacy. Up until his untimely death, of course.

Karrev rubbed his forehead. How would the master have gotten the substance aboard? He could have bribed the inspectors of course, but the price would have been extremely high, and addicts avoided paying for anything other than their addiction, hence the bare room.

If Loba hadn't paid a bribe, he would have hidden a bottle and needles in something made of a dense material that would fool the scanners.

Karrev's gaze travelled the room once more. Peeking out from under some crumpled bedclothes was the edge of a black box. He'd already inspected the box closely for an opening, but he'd found nothing, and he'd tossed it to the floor in favor of more promising objects. It was so plain, so simple...so easily overlooked.

Reaching over, he pulled the box from under the sheets.

Squinting in the low light, Karrev examined it again. This was definitely it. It had to be. There was nowhere left to search. But how did it open? Beginning at one edge, Karrev pressed the box's surface, painstakingly working his way across it, leaving no part unexplored. He was over halfway through his experiment before he was finally rewarded. He applied pressure in an area that looked no different from the rest, and like fruit cleaving under a knife, the box opened.

Karrev's hand trembled. He had to grab the box with his other hand to prevent himself from dropping the precious find. Within the box's center, alongside a set of hollow silver needles, was a bottle of vivid crimson liquid.

Karrev had never set eyes on mythranil before. His upbringing had barely afforded him the cheapest of drugs. But he'd heard all about it. The name everyone used for it—myth—suited it well. The drug was legendary in its reputation. A single drop of myth, it was said, gave you a run so good you'd kill your own mother for another. And here he was with a whole bottle of it right there in his hand, worth enough for a deposit on a starship.

The door to the cabin began to slide open. Karrev snapped the box shut and shoved it under the bed sheets. Micah, a fellow lab tech, looked in. He jumped a little when he saw Karrev. The man grinned sheepishly. "You had the same idea as me, then."

"Dunno what you mean," replied Karrev, trying to sound casual as he got to his feet.

Micah stepped into the room and surveyed the results of Karrev's search. "Come on, you've obviously torn this place apart. Find anything good?" He looked Karrev up and down, his gaze dwelling on the flat pockets of the man's uniform. His left eyebrow lifted quizzically.

Karrev gave a small chuckle. "Ah, you got me." He

slapped Micah on the back. "Why shouldn't we help ourselves, though? If it wasn't us doing it, it would be someone else, right? Who knows how long it's going to take Polestar to rescue us? We've got to look after ourselves."

Micah also laughed. "That's right. Nothing wrong with looking out for number one. It isn't like the owners are coming back, is it?" His smile faded, and he looked Karrev in the eye. "So, what did you find?"

Spreading his hands wide, Karrev replied, "Not a thing. Searched everywhere, as you can see. You'd think, with him being a master, there'd be plenty, but...nothing. I can't figure it out. Maybe someone thought of it sooner."

Micah held Karrev's gaze a few moments before frowning at the trashed cabin. "I might have a look myself."

"Go ahead," said Karrev. "Let me know if you find anything. I'd be interested. But I've had enough of this. I'm going to check out Lee's cabin. Her family were loaded, I heard."

"But she isn't dead."

"Dead, in stasis, it's all the same, isn't it? And if they do bring her back, I don't think she's going to be asking about her genuine wool bedspread or whatever, is she?" He went to the door. "Good luck. Like I said, let me know what you find."

Micah hesitated. "No, wait, I'm coming with you. Looks like you did a thorough job on this place. You're right. Lee's cabin's a better prospect."

"Now hold on a minute. That was my idea. I didn't say I was going to share her stuff. I wish I hadn't mentioned it now."

"Fair's fair, Karrev, what's in her cabin isn't any more yours than mine. Look, I promise I won't tell another soul, and we'll split it all fifty—fifty."

Karrev's eyebrows rose.

"Sixty—forty then."

Karrev's eyebrows rose higher.

"All right, all right. Seventy—thirty."

Shaking his head, Karrev said, "I've always been too soft. Come on." As Micah left the room, Karrev took a last look, his gaze resting momentarily on the bump beneath the sheets. What wouldn't he give to retrieve that box right now. After all the effort he'd put into finding it, the myth was his and his alone. But he couldn't risk Micah knowing about it. He would have to be patient.

When he could slip away unnoticed, he would come back and get it, and then...The possibilities rose before him like angels ascending to heaven. What or who was there aboard that he couldn't buy for a drop of myth? Who was there that he couldn't compel to do his bidding?

All his life Karrev had been last in line, bottom of the pile, looked down upon, forgotten, taken for granted, taken advantage of. Now, through his smarts and hard work, he'd finally turned the tables. Now, it was going to be his turn.

5

———

As Jas shut down the interface screen and stood up, she concluded that going over the supply list had been even more tedious than she'd imagined it would be. The numbers didn't mean anything to her by themselves anyway. She needed to know what they meant. Jas set off to the storeroom to speak to the second steward. The chief steward had been infected and had died during the crash-landing, but his subordinate seemed organized and dependable.

She found the man snapping open the locks on the lid of a box. He looked up as she entered.

"I thought you might be over," he said. "You got the report I sent?"

"I've just finished reading it. Things don't seem too bad, providing the crew love freeze-dried sweet potato powder."

The second steward smiled. "I believe it was one of the master's favorites. We seem to have a lot of it."

"I've come to ask you, what does it all mean in terms of day-to-day supplies? How long do we have before we run out of food?"

"I've been working it out. I calculate that, at the current rate of consumption, we have about two months. But the ship's cooling. I've already had to put on extra clothes to stay warm. When the temperature has equalized with what it is outdoors, people will need to eat more. So if we don't get the heating going, you can take a week or two off that estimate. That's without cutting down on calories, though. If we put the crew on starvation rations today—"

Jas raised a hand. She didn't even want to think about that. Two months. It didn't seem a very long time, but it was long enough to find out if they could fix the engines; it was long enough for a rescue ship, if one was coming.

"If we could get the waste treatment system working again," continued the steward, "we could last longer—much longer. No one likes eating the nutrient bricks, but they do supply the necessary calories. And we could convert many inedible items to nutrients. Anything that was once organic. If we could power up the waste treatment...?" He looked hopefully at Jas.

She sighed. Power. It always came down to the same thing. Power for heat, water, lighting, food, repairs, comm, everything. Up until then, they'd been running on emergency power. She didn't know if they could reinstate the power supply from the engines. That was another job for MacAdam. If they couldn't, it looked like they had two months before things got bad.

Then again, if the engines couldn't supply power, it would mean they were beyond repair, and it would just be a matter of surviving as long as they could.

She realized the second steward was watching her. "Sorry. Thanks for figuring all that out."

The man shrugged. "It's my job, whether the ship's flying or not."

"How are you getting the food out to the crew?"

"I've allotted a daily ration to each person. They've formed themselves into groups, and usually one person comes and collects that day's ration for their group."

"And do you think they're sharing out the food fairly?"

"I think so. No one seems worried about food supplies yet. I haven't heard any complaints. People understand it's an emergency situation. I don't know how long that'll last, though.

"I use the chief steward's office to dispense the food. I didn't think it would be wise for them to see the amount of supplies we have, especially if stocks begin to run low."

"I agree," said Jas, "but I don't like this idea of one person receiving the food for their group. It's too open to exploitation. What if someone decides someone else doesn't deserve their food, or demands favors before they hand it out? No. Let's make it so that each person collects their own food. I know it'll take longer to give it out, but—"

"No, you're right. I'll say it's up to everyone to get their own. I'll make them show their ID and check them off when they collect their rations." The second steward paused and surveyed the storeroom. "I sleep in here, you know. Just in case. I can't lock the door anymore, you see. If the crew starts worrying about the food supply...I'm not sure what I could do if a gang came to help themselves, or to take over the stores and kick me out."

"There's nothing you can do to secure the door?" asked Jas.

"I've tried all kinds of things, but without power..."

They were back to power again.

"I could barricade it, I suppose," continued the second steward. "But then I'd have to take the barricade down every morning and put it up every night. And anyone who was determined enough could break it down."

Jas sighed. "How about if you had a defense unit outside the door round the clock?" She had a limited supply of units and defense concerns of her own. She had them stationed at the ship's exit hatches, where they should be—protecting the crew from outsiders. The second steward's worries weren't a surprise to her, but devoting a unit to protect food supplies seemed a waste. The crew shouldn't need protecting from themselves. But the man had a point. If someone got control of the supplies, they would have control of the entire ship.

"A defense unit outside the room would certainly keep people away," said the steward, "but it might also increase fears about the supplies running out. I'll take up your offer, but I'll keep the unit in here, somewhere out of sight, in case of an emergency."

"Whatever you think best. I'll send one over."

Leaving the second steward to his inventory, she went to find MacAdam. The woman was supposed to have brought her a report on the state of the engines, but she hadn't shown up. It was strange. She had to have finished by now, but she hadn't come to the bridge as ordered. Jas would have to go and find her. She needed to know if there was any hope of them leaving the planet by themselves.

MacAdam wasn't in the canteen, nor any of the communal areas. Jas asked around, and eventually other crew members directed her to the engineer's cabin, though they had odd expressions on their faces that Jas couldn't understand. When she pushed open the door to the room, the reason for their expressions was soon apparent. The place stank of alcohol. Ship-distilled gut rot.

It was a narrow, mean room, containing little more than

four bunks and accompanying interfaces and cupboards. MacAdam was the cabin's only occupant. The woman was on one of the top bunks, flat on her back and snoring, an arm and leg hanging lazily down.

A slow rage began to build in Jas. Here she was with the responsibility of nearly two hundred lives on her shoulders, two hundred people who she might have to watch die because she couldn't help them, and this woman, this woman who was supposed to be such a brilliant mechanic, who had just one job... She strode over to MacAdam, grabbed the front of the engineer's uniform and, with some effort, shook her awake.

MacAdam's eyes opened halfway, then went wider as she caught sight of Jas's angry face. Her mouth worked as if she were about to speak, but instead of words coming out, she coughed and retched. Jas wasn't able to get out of the way before sour-smelling vomit poured from the engineer's mouth and down the front of Jas's uniform.

Uttering an exclamation of disgust, the security officer stepped back hastily as MacAdam hung over her bunk and threw up again, the thin liquid splashing to the floor. Jas raised the back of her wrist to her mouth and wrinkled her nose. "For krat's sake," she spat. "What the hell do you think you're doing, woman?"

MacAdam clung to the side of her bunk, as if worried she would fall. "Sorry," she mumbled. "I fell asleep, and—"

"BF. You didn't fall asleep. You passed out. How much have you drunk, and where did you get it from?"

"I know, I know...sorry...I was just, looking at my, my...and it makes me sad...y'know. Not their fault. S'mine...and—"

"What are you talking about? Did you check the engines? Did you write your report before you decided to get off your legs?"

"I didn't...no point...we've had it. I'll ne'er see them again. Ne'er see them." She flopped back and began weeping.

Jas's anger boiled over. "You're right," she yelled. "No one's going to see anyone again unless we get those engines working. We're relying on you, MacAdam. You're the last engineer on the ship. We need you. We need you sober and working, or we're all dead. Do you understand me? Do you get it?"

Jas continued with her tirade, but the woman's eyes were closing.

The sound of the cabin door opening drew Jas's attention. It was Lingiari.

"I've been looking for you," he said. "I asked around and got sent in this direction. Then I just followed the sound of your voice."

"Look at her," exclaimed Jas. "Our last kratting hope. Off her legs."

"Yeah, well, I don't think she can hear you anymore, even if the rest of the ship can, so maybe you should rein it in?"

Jas took a deep breath and closed her eyes. She opened them again and said, "What did you want to see me about?"

"You know how we were wondering if Lee had managed to send a packet to Earth? Sparks says we can ask her ourselves."

6

Karrev tried to time his return to Loba's cabin to the quiet shift, but the shift system was breaking down, and random patterns of work, sleep, and eating had developed. He picked the time when fewest people seemed to be up and around, and set off, weighing up his chances of being observed against those of someone else discovering Loba's secret stash of bliss before he could collect his find.

As he pushed open the cabin door, he thought something looked different about the room, but he couldn't figure out what. It was just as messy as when he'd left it, so it was difficult to tell if anything had been moved or disturbed. But it didn't matter, even if Micah or someone else had been searching. Karrev had spotted the edge of Loba's strange black box sticking out from under the pile of sheets.

He stooped and picked it up. He'd memorized exactly where to press the box to make it open. His heart thudded as the lid lifted. The bottle of mythranil lay, deep crimson, in the center. He basked in the glory of his treasure for a moment before the closet door flew open and a figure sprang out and crashed into him, propelling the box from his hands. Karrev let out a scream of rage that was cut off as he hit the floor. His assailant—Micah—dove on top of him. The black box landed upside down, and Karrev's fingers scrabbled for it, fighting the weight on his chest.

"I knew it," came Micah's voice in his ear. "I knew there was something in here you were hiding. So what is it?"

Karrev was freed as the other man dashed for the box. Micah gasped as he picked it up and saw what lay on the floor beneath it: scattered silver needles and the bottle of myth, miraculously unharmed.

Micah's voice was reverent. "Is that—"

Karrev rose in a rage and flew at Micah as he reached for the myth. He knocked the man violently against the wall. The box fell from his grasp. Pressing him against the wall, Karrev fastened his hands around Micah's throat, but he had a bull's neck, and he tensed his muscles, fighting Karrev's chokehold as he pulled on his arms. The two men struggled, Karrev trying to choke Micah, Micah fighting to free himself from Karrev's grasp. Micah's eyes were wide and staring, and the veins stood out on his forehead. The men struggled silently.

Micah drove his knee between Karrev's legs, and pain exploded from the man's groin to his stomach. Karrev collapsed, gripping his genitals, immobilized with agony.

Rubbing his throat, Micah coughed harshly. He scanned the floor until he spied the bottle of mythranil. He picked it up with a gentleness that contrasted his large frame. Seemingly mesmerized, he held the bottle up to the meager light and gazed at the contents.

"Never seen it before," he said, as if to himself. "Heard plenty, but never seen it. I wonder if it's as good as they say."

Water pouring from his eyes and nose, Karrev was

regaining some control. He pulled his knees beneath himself so that he was kneeling, one hand resting on the floor, the other gently nursing his groin. He squinted up at Micah. "I'll go fifty—fifty with you," he growled.

"Ha, you're not in much of a position to be bargaining."

"I found it. I pulled this place apart. I figured out where it was. I got the box open. It should be mine, by rights."

"Not from where I'm standing." Micah pulled open the front of his uniform as if looking for somewhere safe to stow the bottle.

"Sixty—forty, then," said Karrev, his breathing easing as the waves of pain from his stomach subsided a little.

Micah looked down his nose at the crouching man. "Why should I give you anything?"

"Thirty—seventy."

Micah snorted a laugh and took a step toward the door. Karrev stood up. The heavy black box was in his fist. Micah paused. He took another step to the door.

"Give it to me," said Karrev, holding the box like a weapon. He held out his other hand, palm upward.

Eyelids hooded, Micah edged farther away.

"Give it me," said Karrev, "or so help me, I'll—"

Micah held the bottle out at arm's length. "If you hit me, I'll drop it. From this height, it'll smash. Is that what you want?"

"If I can't have it," roared Karrev, "neither of us can." He flew at Micah. The man raised his arm but couldn't move fast enough to ward off the blow. The box struck his head with a hollow thunk, and the bottle of mythranil fell. Karrev dove and caught it before it hit the floor. Micah staggered, blood leaking from his wound.

Karrev carefully placed the bottle at the edge of the room, out of danger, before returning to the stricken Micah.

He hit him again with the box, sending him to the floor. Karrev hit him again and again, spattering the man's blood over himself. Micah's skull shattered. It wasn't until Karrev glimpsed the man's brain that he paused, panting, his arm aching.

He drew himself upright and wiped a sleeve across his face, smearing the blood and mixing it with his sweat. He listened for sounds from outside for a moment, but none came. Apparently, no one had heard the fight. The ache from his genitals began to register once more. He limped over to the bottle of myth, picked it up, and put it in his pocket. Then he gathered Loba's sheet and used it to wipe off Micah's blood from his skin and clothes as best he could.

As he tossed the sheet down, he took another brief survey of the room. He scooped up the scattered needles, tore off a piece of cloth and wrapped them with it before putting them in another pocket.

Micah's body gave a convulsive twitch, and he released a long breath. Then he was utterly still. Karrev scowled at the man's ruined face. "Thirty—seventy, pah." He spat on Micah's upturned eyes.

Lee looked almost alive in the coffin-like stasis container. The injury that had as good as killed her was a trauma to the back of her skull. Her brain had swollen, and her heart and breathing had stopped, Sparks explained to Jas. The internal pressure from the swelling and the lack of oxygen had severely damaged Lee's brain. Stasis kept her bodily functions going artificially, albeit at an extremely slow rate, so that what remained of the brain tissue wouldn't deteriorate further. Her skin retained its plumpness, though it was pale, and if Jas ignored the fact that she wasn't breathing, Lee looked like she was in a very deep sleep.

It was as though Jas could reach out a hand and wake her up.

The doctor was fitting electrodes to Lee's skull, pushing aside her cropped blonde hair, and fixing tiny circles of thin plastic to her scalp.

"It looks so twenty-first century," said Lingiari. "You sure it'll work?"

"If there's anything left of her mind, we should get some

kind of response," replied Sparks, "though what exactly, I don't know. I've never done this before. It was only a small part of my training, because there's little use for this on Earth, of course. There, we would immediately read and store whatever was left of the patient's mind, to be ready for uploading to a clone, if the family could pay. But here, with no cloning facilities, we have to retain as much of Lee as we can for as long as we can. I don't know exactly what's there. My scanner isn't sensitive enough to read low-level brain activity, hence the electrodes."

He placed the final one, "There," he said and stepped back. He turned to a control panel. "Now, let's see—"

"Wait a minute," said Jas, placing a hand on the man's arm as he reached to press the screen. "What are we actually doing here? I mean, are we just listening in?" If they couldn't talk to Lee, it might take hours to hear the answers to their questions. Meanwhile, they would hear what was going on in her brain, things she might prefer that they didn't know.

"It really depends on what's left," replied Sparks. "Lee's mind was exceptional—highly modded, highly developed, which increases the chances of some parts of it surviving. Like spilling water from a container, to put it crudely. Most of us carry a couple of cups of water. A severe injury like this would mean both cups are empty. But Lee's mind was like a bowl. She had water to spare." He reached for the panel. "The electrodes will both stimulate her brain and read the activity in whatever remains of her mind."

A knot formed in Jas's stomach. Lingiari was standing on the other side of the receptacle where Lee was lying. The pilot's features were clouded. He and Lee had grown close in their fight for control of the ship.

"But, what I want to know is," insisted Jas, "will we be able to talk to her? And if we can, how will she understand?

Will she know where she is? Will we have to tell her what's happened?"

Sparks shook his head. "I just can't tell you for sure. I really have very little experience with this. I'd forgotten that accessing the mind of the person in stasis was a possibility. It was only when I saw that Pilot Lingiari had come to visit and talk to her that I was reminded. So I checked, and the equipment is here. If Lee's auditory nerves are functioning, she will hear us, and she may respond. If not, we may only be able to listen to her thoughts. Of course, the worst case scenario is that we hear nothing."

Lingiari had been visiting Lee? Jas's insides twisted up some more. Yeah, they'd gotten close, but she should have visited her too. She'd been so busy...

Sparks was watching her, waiting for her.

"Go ahead," she said.

The doctor pressed the screen. He, Jas, and Lingiari waited, watching the still figure and listening. Jas wondered what they were listening for. What did an active mind sound like? Sparks had said they might hear silence. Did the silence mean there was nothing there? Was her mind destroyed? The doctor cleared his throat and nodded at her. He wanted her to speak.

Jas swallowed. "Lee? Can you hear me?"

Nothing.

Lingiari leaned over the prone figure. "Sayen, it's Carl Lingiari." He reached out and gripped her small, perfectly manicured hand. "Don't be scared, okay? You're all right."

A voice came from the speaker. "Carl?" All present except for Lee breathed out, and the collective sigh was audible. But the voice wasn't Lee's voice. It was the digitally generated sound of a random, female voice. It sounded human, but not anything like how Lee had spoken. The hair on the back of Jas's neck stood up. It was like talking to the dead, as if the barrier that divided life from death had distorted Lee's personality, and turned her into something else.

"Yeah, it's Carl. Harrington's here, too, and Dr. Sparks."

"Am I in the medical center? How come I can't see you? Have I gone blind? What happened to me?" Despite the panicked words, Lee's face and body were utterly motionless. The voice was flat and conveyed no emotion.

"Navigator Lee," said Sparks, "I'm sorry to inform you that the *Galathea* crash-landed on the surface of the planet we were surveying. During that crash, you sustained considerable injuries."

"What kind of injuries? What's happened to me?"

Jas waited as the doctor explained to Lee what her injuries were. She was almost grateful that the machine-generated voice didn't express the emotions that impacted Lee one after another as Sparks told her, essentially, that she had died, and that the chances of recovering her personality and memories—of recovering everything that had made her who she was—hung by the finest thread.

Jas found it difficult to look at the dead woman's immobile face as she listened to her talk to the doctor. Her gaze roamed the room, not settling anywhere, especially not meeting Lingiari's eyes. She thought if she looked into the sadness that hung there, she might break.

The doctor finished his explanation, and Lee was quiet.

After a moment's silence, Jas said, "I'm so sorry."

"You don't have anything to apologize for, Harrington," came the electronic voice. "You must have defeated the infected officers if you're here talking to me. You did well. You and Carl saved us."

That wasn't how Jas saw it, but she wasn't about to argue.

"Where have you got me?" Lee asked. "If my injuries are so bad, how come I can talk to you? I feel weird."

"You're in the stasis room," replied Lingiari. "We're keeping you alive, and we're going to take you back to Earth, where they can help you. We'll fix the engines, or we'll get rescued. We're not—"

"Is it clean?"

"What?" asked Jas.

"I must be in a stasis container. There isn't any dust or anything, is there? I can't stand dirt. I don't want to be lying in some dirty box."

Jas laughed. "Yeah, it's pretty clean."

"Pretty clean isn't good enough. Can you get someone to wipe it out for me? I've got some sanitized wipes in my cabin."

Lingiari was laughing now, too.

"I'm glad y'all find it so funny. Hey, what I can't figure out is, why did you wake me up? Must be pretty creepy talking to a body."

"You're right. We did wake you up for a reason," said Jas. "We need to know something. That packet I asked you to send to Earth, telling them what was happening. Did you manage to send it?"

"I sure did. Got it off right before we crashed. I included everything. About Loba, Margret, and the officers, and K. 67092d. I told them everything. It took me a while, and I didn't have time to get to my crash seat before we hit."

Jas and Lingiari locked eyes. If Lee had sent the packet, that meant Earth had had plenty of time to reply. But no message had come as far as they knew.

"Is there anything else you want to know?" asked Lee.

"Not right now," replied Jas, "but we might need your

help. Is it okay to wake you up to talk to you like this? Or would you prefer to sleep until we get you back to Earth?"

"I'd like you to wake me up and speak to me whenever you can, even if you don't have anything to ask me. It's kinda lonely here."

Jas recalled how the navigator had been the only one to come to her room when Loba had confined her to her cabin, and how chatty she'd been. "I'll come talk to you whenever I can."

"So will I," said Lingiari.

Sparks left them alone as they spent the next half hour bringing the navigator up to speed on everything that had happened since the crash-landing. When no one had anything else to say, Jas asked her if she wanted them to turn off the electrodes until next time.

"No, leave them on," replied Lee. "I'd like to think a while.

8

———

J as awaited MacAdam's arrival at the mission room, which remained a meeting and planning place during the emergency situation. It was the only part of the ship apart from the bridge where the emergency power extended to computer access.

Jas had asked the engineer to meet with her to give a full verbal report on the state of the engines, but she had another reason for requesting a one-to-one with the engineer. She hadn't yet gotten over her shock at finding the woman drunk. Jas wasn't naive. Though she didn't take part in the alcohol and drug abuse that everyone knew went on aboard the ship—a minor part of her job was to try to keep it under control, in fact—she couldn't comprehend what had gotten into the engineer's head that she'd thought it was an acceptable alternative to reporting on the state of the engines. It was beyond her comprehension that someone who had everyone relying on her would mess up so badly.

But Jas also knew she hadn't handled the situation well, and she needed to put that right. Losing her cool like that hadn't been the reaction of a good master. What was more,

MacAdam was possibly *the* most important person aboard the *Galathea*. Her judgment and capabilities had to be unimpaired, and that meant Jas had to treat her with kid gloves. She had to make the woman understand how important she was, but not put so much pressure on her that she needed to escape.

While waiting for the engineer to arrive, Jas switched on the hologram of K. 67092d. She recalled the last view she'd had of the image, when Loba had been quizzing her as to why she wouldn't give the all-clear to Resource Assess the surface. That moment seemed like a long time ago.

A cough caught her attention. MacAdam had arrived and was waiting in the doorway. Jas had a feeling it was the second time she'd coughed.

"Thanks for coming. Sit down."

The woman took a seat on the other side of the horizontal screen that displayed the spinning globe. Jas switched it off and took another seat. Everyone looked ill in the ghostly emergency light, but the engineer looked particularly bad. Her cheeks and eyes were hollow and shadowed. Jas could almost make out the shape of her bony skull beneath her ginger curls. An acne spot flared almost comically at the end of her snub nose.

Jas had expected MacAdam to offer an apology for her behavior, but none seemed forthcoming. The engineer didn't meet her eyes. An angry rebuke rose to Jas's lips, but she bit her tongue. "What can you tell me about the engines? Did you complete a full survey?"

"I did. I tested each part. The upper levels have normal function according to the readouts, but I didn't get much information about the lower halves of the engines. It's to be expected. Judging by what the impact did to the engine housing, both the starjump and RaptorX engines are damaged, as far as I can tell."

"So, do you know what's broken, and the minimum we need to fix to get them working again? Can we cannibalize the upper levels for replacement parts?"

MacAdam shrugged. "I only know how to do diagnostic checks and some servicing and maintenance. I don't have a good idea of how each part functions. Engineers train for six years, and this was my first year." The woman glanced up. "Is there any news on a rescue?"

Jas rubbed between her eyebrows. "Please don't say anything to the rest of the crew, but we can't rely on being rescued. We might have to make it out of here ourselves, and we need more information on the engines than the function readouts."

MacAdam studied the backs of her hands. "I understand, but what can I do?"

You could start by not getting off your legs. "I was disappointed to find you drunk in your cabin yesterday. You understand that alcohol and all other drugs are banned aboard ship? You know that, right?"

The engineer was silent.

Jas wished the woman would meet her halfway at least, not this silence. What did it mean? She couldn't figure her out. She wished she was back with her defense units, who were much easier to understand than people. "MacAdam, I know there's a lot of pressure on you right now. When you signed up, you didn't know we would crash or that you would be the last engineer on board, with all of us depending on you. But I can't help that. No one can. It's just how it is. But I can try to help. If it ever feels too much...if you ever feel the need for someone to talk to...Dr. Sparks can offer counseling." Jas's stomach turned at the thought of sending the woman to the bigoted quack, but she had to admit he did have people skills.

The engineer's head was still down, and she was slowly shaking it. Tears splashed on her hands, which lay folded in her lap. Jas felt for her, but she didn't know what she could do to help the woman's situation. MacAdam was saying something.

"What?" asked Jas.

"I said, I'll do my best."

"Thanks, MacAdam. I appreciate it. We all do. You can access the ship's databanks in this room. They contain the engine schematics. Feel free to come here whenever you want, and whatever help you need, just let me know, okay?"

The engineer nodded but didn't raise her head. The woman seemed so crushed, so sad. Jas got the feeling there was more to her problems than the pressure she was under to fix the engines. "MacAdam, is there anything else I should know?"

"No...I, I'll study the schematics."

"And if you need a defense unit for some heavy lifting, I've got one or two to spare."

"It's okay. We—I—have my own equipment for that."

"Right, come over here, then." Jas took her across to an interface where she could access the database. After she'd shown the engineer how to retrieve the information, she returned to the hologram screen and switched on the image of K. 67092d. She wondered how much danger they were in from the planet's inhabitants. They'd crashed near one of the planet's poles, in an area that hadn't been close-scanned or RA'd. Not that it would have made much difference. They hadn't found anything that had seemed dangerous before, yet look at them now.

Jas's mind returned to the structure she'd seen when

they'd disposed of the officers' bodies. It had seemed identical to all the others. Something in those structures infected people with an alien life form that took possession of them. But the answer as to what those things were, and how they operated, eluded her. Were they going to come out and attack their sitting-duck ship? If possessed officers remained on board—maybe someone like Haggardy—would they try to retrieve them?

Leaning over her data screen, MacAdam gave a satisfied *hmpf*.

"Have you found something?" asked Jas.

"No, but I've found out how I might be able to find something."

"Huh?"

"I just noticed the ship's scanners are still operating. They weren't affected by the crash-landing, though the computer isn't logging the information. I think I can turn them a little closer to home and get a detailed scan of the engines. Maybe I can see what's happened down there. If I can find out what's broken, I might be able to figure out how to repair or replace the parts to get the engines working again."

Jas turned to the image of K. 67092d. "What about the rest of the planet? Can you scan the area around us?" The ship's scanners were long-range. Now that they were on the planet surface, maybe they could penetrate deep underground and see what she and the defense units had missed inside the structures.

"I'll try to...doing it," said MacAdam. Jas waited in silence while the scanners did their work. After a few minutes, MacAdam said, "Sending the data over to you."

The hologram of K. 67092d disappeared and was replaced by an image of the planet surface and what lay beneath. The representation was a confused jumble of lines and textures that Jas couldn't interpret at first. The image scrolled slowly across, too large for the screen to display all at once. She plunged her hand into the picture to stop it. She had spotted the *Galathea*.

Everything around them seemed to be innocuous except for the regularly shaped hexagonal blocks, which lay on the surface but also extended far underground. Jas moved her hand to the spot and widened her fingers to expand the area.

MacAdam joined her at the screen. As the hologram zoomed in, something came into view that they both spotted simultaneously. "What's that?" asked MacAdam. Near the base of the artificial structure was a dark blob. Jas closed in on the blob. It looked nothing like the geology surrounding it. Black, vaguely rectangular, and large compared to the nearest block, the image gave no clue as to what it might be.

Jas shrank the hologram until they could see the *Galathea*, the hexagonal structures, and the button-sized blob beneath it. According to the hologram readout, the structure was about twenty kilometers away, and the blob was a hundred meters below the surface.

With a handful of defense units, Jas could get to it and find out what it was.

9

Outside the *Galathea's* access hatch, the sky was lightening with the approaching sun. Jas looked down the side of the ship. It was a long, long drop to the ground, where she could make out the remains of the body bags they'd thrown out a few days earlier. Strapped to the back of a defense unit, she should be safe enough on the trip to the surface. The units could climb up or down anything, gripping with specially textured hands and boots.

If only Lingiari weren't being so difficult about it. The expedition made perfect sense to her, but he wouldn't stop glaring, and with that animal sitting on his shoulder, she was having difficulty taking his objections seriously.

"What if you don't make it back, huh?" asked the pilot. "What happens then? You're in charge of the ship." His pet, Flux, was preening his bat-like, transparent wings, messing up the man's hair.

"Lingiari, it isn't like this is my first time. I know what I'm doing. If anyone should go and investigate that structure, and maybe find the aliens that infected those officers, it should be me. If I don't come back—which is very, very unlikely—someone else will have to take over. Whoever's next in command." Jas looked upward as she took a moment to figure out who that was. "Which is you."

The pilot had his hands on his jutting hipbones, where his uniform trousers clung to his rangy frame. An earring curved from one ear, and his sugar glider/bat alien pet was inadvertently pulling his hair over his face. Maybe the man had a point about the next in command. But that couldn't be helped. As long as they were stranded on the planet, they were vulnerable to the alien presence, which had demonstrated its hostility. Knowing *what* they were up against was the best defense they had.

"What makes you think you're going to find what you missed last time?" asked Lingiari.

A pang ran through Jas's conscience. "I've got something to look for now. A target. That thing under the structure has to be important. It's like nothing else I saw in them. Maybe there was another one under the structure where Margret and the others were infected, but the shuttle scanners didn't pick it up."

MacAdam stood by, ready to bolt closed the access hatch as soon as Jas left. The engineer stood silently waiting. The steady, chill wind that seemed to blow everywhere on K. 67092d was making her blink.

Lingiari sighed. "Just promise me you won't do anything different from what you did before. Wear your combat suit, send the defense units ahead—"

"I'm not an idiot, Lingiari."

"Try to stay in contact."

"I'll try. But I'll be okay. I'm sure. I just hope I see something worth the trip."

The pilot seemed to have run out of objections and

reminders. After a last check outside at the barren, empty landscape, and the structure in the distance, Jas climbed into the harness she'd fixed to AX7, and fastened herself in. Feeling like a very large baby in its mother's sling, she commanded the unit to climb out of the access hatch and down to the ground. She had a backpack of supplies in case she had to spend the night on the surface, but she hoped to be back before dark.

The unit maneuvered through the hatch, carrying her on its back. Jas commanded AX12 to follow.

"Good luck," said Flux.

Though Jas had encountered aliens who could communicate in English, she couldn't get used to the creature's Australian accent. "Err...thanks."

"Lee says good luck, too," said Lingiari.

AX7 began to work its way down the metal skin of the starship.

"You've been talking to her?" There was that strange feeling twisting in her stomach again.

Lingiari leaned out of the hatch and looked down at her. "She likes the company."

Jas had meant to go and spend some time with Lee, too, but she'd had so much to do. "Great. Say hi for me." She had an afterthought. "And ask her if she can think of anything, any ideas that might help us."

"Yeah, she's already working on it." The pilot's head and shoulders were silhouetted against the brightening morning sky.

AX7 developed a steady rhythm as it climbed down the ship's side, its movements sure and steady. Jas rested her forehead against the android's broad back. Its skin and combat suit were one and the same thing, which meant that, though the androids were part-organic, no warmth radiated from them. Nonetheless, Jas found the smooth surface oddly soothing. She closed her eyes and waited for AX7 to reach the ground.

After a short while, she looked up toward the access hatch. Lingiari had gone, and the hatch was closed. Jas was uneasy at leaving the crew alone, even with defense units to protect them, but she'd decided that not knowing what faced them was a greater threat.

The planet's sun rose as Jas and the units descended. When she finally reached the surface, Jas did her best to ignore the blackened remains of the officers' bodies. Though in one sense, she was relieved that they were still there. She'd feared that, zombie-like, they might rise from the dead, the aliens that had inhabited them somehow re-animating the burnt corpses.

The two defense units set off. As they ran, Jas wondered what the creatures that had possessed the officers looked like. If they could inhabit another species, were they some kind of liquid that could enter and take up residence in the brain and nervous system? Or were they a powder that the officers had unknowingly breathed in? Her experiences with the alien life forms she'd encountered so far had taught her that, no matter what her expectations were, reality would exceed them.

By the time she and the units had arrived at the struc-ture, Jas was sore from AX7's jarring gait. She gratefully unclipped herself and slid to the ground. After taking a moment to stretch and return the sensation to her numb extremities, she lowered the visor on her helmet and instructed the defense units to ready their weapons and enter, assess, and survey. They went in. When they gave the all-clear, Jas followed.

She went after them as they cleared each empty room in

turn and progressed deeper into the structure. Lacking the units' tracking function, she realized that any humans who traveled through the many rooms within the building would become seriously lost. But none of the RA teams were supposed to have done more than check out the exteriors. That had been her recommendation. Unless Loba had ignored even that?

Her headlight had switched itself on, and along with the defense units,' it swept the bare, dark gray walls. Her auditory system was picking up no noise other than the tramp of their boots. She brought up the ship's scanner image on the interior of her visor, showing the path to where the dark blob lay beneath them. It grew larger and drifted in and out of view as they worked their way toward it.

It wasn't until they were quite close that she realized *how* much larger it was than the rooms they were passing through. The dark blob loomed massively on her screen. It was only a representation of the recording, so the details didn't become more refined the closer they got.

Finally, she understood that the blob must lie in the next room. Her muscles tensed.

She waited, listening. No sound or light came through the entrance. She told the defense units to ready their weapons. AX7 went in, followed by AX12.

"All clear, C.S.O Harrington."

Jas stepped through.

The thing that lay before her was only partially exposed. One side of it protruded from broken rock. They had reached the very bottom of the structure, and the gray walls had finally disappeared. They were in some kind of cavern.

She went over to the thing she'd been seeking. It looked so out of place in that underground environment that it took her some time to recognize it for what it was. She ran a gloved hand over the surface. It was ridged and metallic, and at one time it had probably been very strong. The species that had created it must have been visual, she realized, as there were many reinforced windows giving tantalizing glimpses of the interior.

" AX7," said Jas, "can you comm a unit aboard the Galathea?"

"No, C.S.O. Harrington. We are down too deep. I have not been able to contact defense units aboard the *Galathea* for some time."

Jas would have to wait until she returned to the surface to tell the others that she'd found what looked like the remains of an alien starship.

10

———

Karrev had stolen a fancy, pure silk bag in which to carry the bottle of mythranil, but that was the least of his work since securing the drug as his, and his alone. He'd made sure that Micah had an unfortunate accident in the engine. Dr. Sparks's tests on what remained of the body had found alcohol in his blood, so it wasn't difficult to conclude that the man had climbed into an engine access hatch while intoxicated, and slipped and fallen.

Karrev had also bribed two guards with a couple of drops of the precious myth for access to the small armory. He'd passed two of the weapons he purloined to a couple of burly friends and promised them a once-a-month run in return for their services. The rest of the weapons were to be distributed to those who would go along with his plan.

Now, he had to get the support of a sizeable proportion of the crew. Most of them were like him—only basically modded, or even naturals. Shut out of the circles in which society's elites moved, their hard lives were made more bearable by regularly resorting to narcotics. They would be familiar with the rumors about myth, though few would have had the money or opportunity to try it. He could offer them the prospect of hours of bliss in return for simply switching allegiance from their current masters to him.

And now that Harrington was off the ship, it should be simple to take control.

He'd put out the word: anyone who was unhappy with the current situation was to meet in the auditorium at a certain hour. Karrev hadn't been surprised when he saw the large turnout. Morale was low. There'd been no mention of getting off the planet, or a rescue ship. All they'd heard from the higher-ups was work, work, work; do this, do that. Meanwhile, it was getting colder, and everyone knew the food wouldn't last forever.

When it looked like no one else was coming, Karrev stepped up to the podium and ordered that the doors be shut. The room buzzed. He held up a hand for silence. He would let his greatest asset do the talking for him. He pulled apart the strings of his bag, reached in, and took out the bottle. As he held it up, the assembled crew members exhaled as one. But Karrev didn't achieve the shock factor he was hoping for. Word had gotten out. "He really does have myth," said a voice. "I never believed it till now."

"You'd better believe it," said Karrev. "I found it in Loba's cabin, locked away in a safe that only I could figure out the combination to." It was simpler than explaining about the box, and Karrev had kept it to store the myth in while he slept.

"*Found*," someone said. "That's a good way of putting it."

Karrev smiled. "It was there for the taking. Finders keepers, as they say. But it can be yours, too, if you follow me."

The shipmates Karrev had persuaded to be his body-guards stood on either side of him, gripping their weapons.

"I don't know," said an older woman. "Even if it is myth, that doesn't mean we should do what you say."

"Haven't you heard what this stuff does?" a member of the audience retorted. "A few tiny drops is worth a mission bonus to the likes of us. What must the run be like? Use your imagination."

"Yeah, I'm too old for all that. Keep your drugs. I'm going to bed." The woman walked off, and the rest of the audience shifted restlessly.

A hand rose. It was the hand of a short, round man, who was a sanitation worker. "I used to deal in such things. I've sold myth in my time, though I've never seen so much all at once. Could I have a look?"

Karrev hesitated. He'd assumed the stuff was myth, or else why would Loba have hidden it so well? But he didn't know for sure. If he didn't let the man look at it, however, he would lose all credibility.

"'Course. Come up here. Help yourself," he said expansively.

The crowd opened to let the man through. Reluctance gripping him, Karrev handed over the bottle. The man held it up to the light before turning it on its side and watching the liquid as it flowed. Lastly, he opened the bottle and held it under his nose. Closing his eyes, he sniffed deeply. Immediately, he staggered, and Karrev snatched the bottle from him. He firmly screwed the lid on and frowned.

The man's eyes glazed over. They rolled back in his head, and he collapsed gracefully, his knees leading the way, followed by his tubby body and limp arms. A few hands half-heartedly caught him and broke his fall.

Karrev said nothing, allowing the spectacle of the

chubby man to speak for him. He raised the myth in his right hand, and the crowd cheered. As the shouts and whoops died away, he cut through the fading noise. "If you want a taste of this, you do what I say, right?"

The audience gave their assent loudly.

"First," said Karrev, "we take the ship!"

11

Sayen looked identical to how she'd been when Carl had last left her. Cushioned on a water-filled base in her stasis container, which undulated gently to help prevent pressure sores, she lay under a sheet. Beneath the sheet, tubes had been inserted into her body to maintain its temperature and systems at a level that kept her just alive. Her arms were above the sheet, with her palms face down, and her head was resting to one side. Her mouth was slightly open, and a thin line of drool ran from the corner.

Carl pulled his sleeve over his hand and wiped the spittle away. Sayen's hair was growing out of its short-cropped style. He felt like he'd got to know the woman better in the last few days than he had in all the previous months aboard ship. Her exclusive modding, private schooling, and privileged upbringing in her family's large home in the southern United States among nannies and servants could not have contrasted more with his rough-and-tumble childhood in rural New South Wales, Australia.

Sayen had told the pilot many stories, such as tales of dinner parties her parents had held, where they'd served strange, imported, alien foods to impress their wealthy guests. Sayen had been expected to try each of them without making a face, probably to demonstrate to her parents' friends how sophisticated she was, when really her favorite thing to eat was a PBJ sandwich. Other stories recalled the amazing trips she'd taken, like the time she'd flown in her parents' private jet to the beach just for the day, only to be told she couldn't play in the sand in case she got dirty or hurt herself.

In turn, Carl had related his childhood tales—how his first memory was of flying, strapped into his dad's twin-engine. He could remember his dad's head outlined against a brilliant blue sky, the roar of the engine, and the wind taking his breath from him. His second memory was of sitting on a horse's back, gripping its mane in chubby fingers, while his mum walked it on a lead around the paddock. All his childhood, he seemed to have been moving in one way or another. Telling Sayen about it all had brought back the memories vividly. He'd felt a sudden urge to see his parents' sunburned, wrinkled faces again and feel the hot Australian sun on his back.

"Are you still there, Carl?" came the electronic voice that conveyed Sayen's thoughts.

"Yeah, sorry, I drifted off for a bit. How are you doing?"

"I've been thinking about Harrington's trip to the alien structure and the infection mechanism. You know, I think she'll be okay."

"What makes you think that?" asked Carl.

"Well, we can guess the defense units didn't get infected because they aren't human, but the only difference between the LIVs she conducted and Margret and Loba's encounter with the structures, as far as we know, is that she was wearing a combat suit. Margret and the rest of the RA teams wore Polestar uniforms, which means their skin was exposed. I'm wondering if it's something to do with physical contact with one of the alien buildings. If someone touches a structure, maybe it triggers a reaction, reads their DNA, which results in the infection. If I'm right, providing she stays suited up, she should be safe."

"That makes sense. I'll comm her to tell her. Do you think I can speak to her through one of the defense units in here powering your stasis?"

"I reckon so."

Carl went to the nearest unit to read its designation. "AX1, can you comm one of the units out with Harrington?"

"Pilot Lingiari, do you mean can I communicate with AX7 or AX12?"

"Yeah. Could you tell them to pass her a message?"

"I can. Would you like me to comm AX7 or AX12?"

"AX7'll do. Tell it to tell Harrington not to take off her combat suit. She shouldn't touch the walls with her bare skin. Can you ask it to tell her that?"

"Do not take off your combat suit. Do not touch walls with your bare skin. Is that the message?"

"Yep, that's it."

Flux swept into the room. "Lingiari, you better get out. There's trouble on the way, mate."

Shouts and laughter came from the corridor.

"Urgent report, Pilot Lingiari," said AX1.

"What's going on?" asked Sayen.

"What's happening, AX1?" Carl asked.

"Weapons have been discharged in the storeroom, on the bridge, and in the living quarters. Units are awaiting instructions."

"What?" *Krat.* "AX1, tell the units to go to the conflict

areas and…I don't know, stun the fighters. Anyone holding a weapon. Except each other."

"Affirmative, Pilot Lingiari." The unit lifted its hands to the cable running from its chest to the stasis unit. The three other units powering the stasis system did the same.

"Whoa, hold on. All units in here, what are you doing?"

"AX1 has relayed your message to all units, and we are going to the nearest conflict area," all four responded at once.

"No, not you guys. Don't disconnect, we need you to power the stasis. All defense units in this room, disregard my previous order."

The units unplugged their cables.

"Wait, what the hell are you doing?" exclaimed Carl.

"Pilot Lingiari, you commanded that we disregard your previous order," said the units. "Your previous order was not to disconnect ourselves, so we have ignored that order."

"Arghhh…NO. All defense units in this room, reconnect your power supply to the stasis system." They did as they were instructed, and Carl closed his eyes in relief. "All units in this room, do not disconnect yourselves, I repeat, DO NOT disconnect yourselves from the stasis system unless it's at my order. Is that clear?"

"Affirmative, Pilot Lingiari," they said. "We will not disconnect ourselves from the stasis system unless we receive a command from an officer ranking higher than pilot."

"Good." It would have to do, and he was the highest ranking officer aboard, wasn't he? Harrington had said so.

12

———

Karrev hadn't included the defense units in his plan, and he regretted it bitterly. His instructions to his followers had been simple: secure the supplies and order anyone who wasn't already his supporter to declare their allegiance to him. If they refused, they were to be brought to him there, in the auditorium, stunned if necessary. He'd planned on taking great pleasure in forcing them to accept him as their new master.

But those great, hulking beasts, more robot than human, couldn't be coerced. The minute that news of his takeover had gotten out, someone had ordered them to squash his rebellion, and they were doing it in their usual efficient style. How could he have been so stupid? Listening to the sounds of weapon fire in the corridors, Karrev took out the bottle of myth and gazed at it. What wouldn't he give to inject just a drop or two and escape this mess he'd created. This wasn't how it was supposed to be.

But myth offered only a temporary answer to his problems. He put the bottle away again in its silk bag. If he wanted to be master of the ship, he needed to think of a way to get control of those units for himself. Then, once they'd gotten the *Galathea* working again, he and his crew could roam the galaxy, discovering new planets, hijacking ships, and taking whatever they wanted. Once he had control of the defense units.

The security officer, Harrington, the one who'd put herself in charge, had gone somewhere, so it wasn't her controlling them. Who else could it be?

Everyone knew that her and the pilot had gotten close. It was they who'd spread the rumor about Loba and the rest of the officers being possessed by aliens. He hadn't believed it for a second. It was too much of a coincidence that most of the officers had been killed when the ship had crashed. It was more likely Harrington and Lingiari had executed them. No one had seen the bodies before they threw them off the ship.

The more he thought about it, the more Karrev realized that his plan to commit mutiny had been nothing of the kind. He was fighting *against* mutineers. He was dispensing justice against Harrington and Lingiari.

He stood up and slung the silk bag around his neck. With newfound enthusiasm, Karrev resolved to continue to fight for control the ship. He would be a hero.

The pilot, Lingiari—that was the one who Harrington must have left in charge. It had to be. If he could find him and kill him, it would be no more than the man deserved, and no one else would command the defense units. No, that was wrong. *He* would command them.

"Hey," he called to one of his bodyguards, who was standing sentry at the auditorium door. "Everyone has to put down their weapons. Spread the word. They have to stop fighting the defense units. I'll send another order later."

The units were only attacking those who put up a fight against them.

After thrusting a weapon into his belt, Karrev left to find Lingiari, taking a couple of bodyguards with him.

His first stop was the mission room. Telling a guard to go first, they went inside. There was no sign of Lingiari. The engineer was the only occupant. She watched him carefully but said nothing. Karrev gave her a curt nod. She would be useful later.

Next, he tried the pilot's sleeping quarters. The room was empty but for that stupid pet of his. Karrev took a shot at it, but it disappeared into a vent. He'd get it next time. He hadn't eaten fresh meat in months. He looked briefly into the shuttle bay, but all that was in there were the melted remains of the shuttle. Where was the man?

"I think I know where he might be," said one of his bodyguards. "The medical center. I heard he goes to visit the dead navigator."

"He does, does he?" replied Karrev. "Must be into corpses. Thanks for the tip."

His guards flanking him, Karrev crept up to the stasis room door, which was slightly open. He could just make out the figure of the pilot. He had his back toward him, and it looked like he was leaning over a long container that had been pulled out from the wall. That had to be where the navigator's body was lying. The man was talking, but he couldn't make out exactly what he was saying. Something about 'worry' and 'ready.'

There didn't seem to be anyone else in the small room. He pulled out his weapon. The glimpse he had of the pilot was too narrow to shoot at accurately, and he might only get one shot. He was about to stride in, flanked by his guards, when a memory, sparked by the bright lights of the room, made him pause.

Soon after the crash, when everything in the ship had been in chaos, he'd heard complaints about the navigator's medical treatment. People had complained that they were using four defense units to power the stasis room, even though the ship needed all the power it could get—even though the navigator was a gonner.

Defense units in the room. *Krat.*

Karrev slid his weapon in his belt. He couldn't kill the pilot until he'd gotten control of the defense units, and he couldn't get control of the defense units until he killed the pilot. He would have to go back to the mission room and try to figure it out.

He hadn't gone far when heavy boots tramped the corridor ahead of him. It was the kind of sound only defense units made, and they were heading his way. Karrev turned and walked quickly in the opposite direction. Could they be after him? Had someone talked? Or had the pilot figured out what he would do? "Come on," he shouted to his guards, and he began to run. Then came the sound of units in front of him. He slowed. He had nowhere to go.

"Shipmate Karrev," came the cool, modulated voice of a unit behind him, "you are under arrest. Stop, or we will shoot you."

He wasn't going to go without a fight. He spun round and aimed, but didn't get a shot out before something exploded against his stomach, and the floor of the corridor came up to meet his face.

When Karrev came around, he was being carried like a sack of meat over a defense unit's shoulder. His nose ached, and blood was dripping from it. He tensed his neck to prevent his nose from banging—he was sure not for the first time—against the unit's back. He lifted his head, but saw nothing but retreating corridor, though he could hear the thump of feet ahead. His guards must have also been stunned, and they were also being carried by units.

Karrev recognized the area of the ship they were in. They were nearly at the brig. Once inside, that would be it for him. Mutiny carried a death penalty. If he was lucky, they would keep him alive until they got back to Earth, but he couldn't afford any fancy attorneys who would tell the true story about what Harrington and Lingiari had done. If he wasn't lucky, well, as soon as Harrington was back that hard bitch probably wouldn't think twice about throwing him off the ship like she had the dead officers.

He wasn't going to give up. There had to be something he could do. He racked his brains, but as he got closer and closer to the brig, no escape plan emerged in his mind.

The bag containing the myth was still hanging from his neck. The stupid unit hadn't even thought to take it off him. Ah well, at least he could spend the time he had left in bliss.

"Karrev?" asked a voice. The unit stopped, and the brig guard walked around it to look at the suspended man. For a moment, Karrev was mildly surprised. He'd forgotten the brig was already guarded; that there were already prisoners in there. Then he remembered who was imprisoned, and his heart stopped.

"What's this?" asked the guard, taking the bag from his neck. The man gasped as he looked inside, and his eyes popped. "I'd heard the rumor, but I didn't believe it." He drew out the bottle and held it up reverently. "AX9, take your prisoner inside," he said without taking his eyes from the crimson liquid.

As the unit carried him and his guards into the four-celled prison, Karrev sought out the prisoner—his method of escape, his Get-Out-of-Jail-Free card. He didn't want to give up control of the ship, but anything was better than this. His gaze alighted on a figure slumped on a bunk.

"Sir," he shouted. "First Mate Haggardy, wake up."

The first mate's eyes opened blearily.

"Sir, quick," continued Karrev, "these units are yours to command. Order them to get you out."

Haggardy's eyes snapped wide. He leapt to his feet as the unit carrying Karrev opened the door to a cell.

"Units, kill the brig guards immediately," Haggardy said. "Unlock my cell. Release me."

Karrev's unit dropped him like a stone, and his skull banged against the floor, momentarily stunning him.

A short time later, when the sparks had stopped firing in his vision and his thoughts cleared, he realized he was still inside his cell, and the door was closed.

He staggered up and went to look into the corridor. The two brig guards were lying facedown, and the smell of burnt flesh hung in the air. Pools of blood were slowly forming beneath them. Haggardy was walking away.

On the guards' table was the bottle of myth, ignored.

13

Toirien had tried. For a little while, she'd been inspired by Harrington. The woman had really seemed to believe she could do it. But she'd given it her best shot, and it wasn't good enough.

Sitting at the screen in the mission room, she sank her head into her hands. She just didn't have the knowledge, nor, she guessed, the intelligence, to understand the engine schematics. She had a basic idea of how the RaptorX engines worked, but while she'd been amazed and impressed at the invention of starjump technology more than twenty years ago, like most people, she'd never really followed the lay explanations the media had published.

It wasn't like she hadn't received basic modding at conception. Her parents hadn't been entirely irresponsible. No, she wasn't dumb, but neither was she bright enough to wrap her head around this technology, at least not without having it taught to her. She realized she'd probably only gotten her job because Polestar had been desperate for recruits.

Her head ached from going over the engine plans and

reading the manuals. She thought she understood better now, but without the chief engineer or someone else to ask, how was she supposed to know if she was right? She couldn't risk starting up the engines. She worried that she could blow up the ship and kill everyone.

So that was it. No one was going home, and it was her fault. She would never see her girls again.

Toirien got up and wandered out of the room. She needed a drink or something stronger, and she needed it fast. She went to her usual supplier, but the man was nowhere to be found. In fact, it occurred to Toirien, the ship seemed strangely empty. She'd heard some kind of commotion earlier, and that goon, Karrev, had broken her concentration when he'd come into the mission room looking for someone. Had she missed something important? Maybe Harrington had come back, and she had some news.

Speeding up her pace, Toirien went to the bridge. It was empty. The canteen was the same. It was dinnertime, and though everyone was making do with rations, most people still congregated in the canteen out of habit. Where had everyone gone?

Eventually, she heard some noises and headed toward the sound. It was coming from the auditorium. There were angry shouts and loud disputes.

Arriving at the scene, she found sixty to seventy crew members in jumbled groups, some lying, some sitting on the floor, some getting physical with each other in minor skirmishes. Ten or fifteen were crowded in a corner. Toirien began to push through them to find out what was so interesting.

"Don't give out so much. There's only a little left. I want my share," came complaints from the group. "It's a waste of time. It's not the real thing. It's a fake. I don't feel anything. Not a thing," others shouted from around the room.

Toirien elbowed more shipmates out of the way, and came upon a couple crouching over a bottle of something. They had tiny droppers, and they were dispensing the bottle's contents into thimble-sized plastic cups. It took Toirien a moment to realize what it was, and the reason for the crew's dissatisfaction. A man received his thimbleful, and tossed it back like a shot.

Misborn. What a waste.

In her long acquaintance with substances that provided an escape from reality, she'd had the privilege of using myth once, just once, but that was enough. The drug had haunted her dreams night and day for months, if not years, after. These idiots didn't understand it had to be injected, not taken by mouth, and it had to be injected at certain points for the full effect.

Myth. A whole bottle. Where had they gotten it from? Who'd managed to smuggle a bottle of myth aboard, and how could they have afforded it? The bottle was nearly empty, but, from the amount of people in the room who seemed to have had some, it must have been full. Someone who lived frugally could retire for life on the cost of that much myth. But, as Toirien knew too well, if you had that much, you were an addict and never thought further than the next run.

She had to have some. Just one more moment of diversion from her misery before a sad, lingering death trapped on that barren planet.

A hand was at the neck of her uniform, dragging her back. She turned and smashed the owner of the hand in her face. The two shipmates in charge of dispensing the myth looked fearful at her violent reaction, and silently handed her a few precious drops.

Holding the cup as steady as if her life depended on it, Toirien went in search of a hypodermic needle and syringe.

~

CARL HATED ARGUING WITH SAYEN, and it felt weird to debate with her blank face and unmoving lips, but he stuck to his guns.

"It's for your own safety," he told her.

"I don't want to be safe. I want to know what's going on. If I'm hooked up, I can hear at least."

"If you're hooked up to electrodes, your container has to be out in the room. Anyone who comes in here can see you. And I can't stay here to protect you. You were right that the ringleader of the mutiny would come here to find me, but it was dangerous. I can't risk leaving you out here alone."

"But why would anyone want to hurt me? I haven't done anyone any harm."

"Sayen, you heard what happened. Things are getting wild out here. I have to put you away." He didn't want to tell her about the resentment the diversion of the defense units' power to the stasis system had caused among the crew.

"Carl, I'm worried that if you disconnect me, that'll be it. No one will wake me up again."

He exhaled. "I know. I get that's what this is about. But I promise, I *promise* I'll wake you up again, and it'll be like you never went to sleep."

No answer came from the stasis' voice. Carl reached over and gently pulled the electrodes from the woman's scalp. Just before he detached the final one, he heard a quiet, "Goodnight, Carl."

He pushed Sayen's container into its slot. As he turned,he saw a figure passing by along the corridor.

"MacAdam," he called. He hadn't seen the engineer all day. He wanted to know if she'd made any progress with the engines.

He waited a few moments, but she didn't return. He went to find her. The door to the medical center was closed, but Carl had a feeling that was where she'd gone. He opened the door and encountered MacAdam making her way out. Her eyes were wide with panic.

"What's wrong? Do you need to see the doctor?" he asked. Recalling that Harrington had found the woman drunk, his first thought was that she might have been trying to find drugs, but they were all well secured, and she hadn't had time to break open the store.

"No," replied MacAdam. "I mean, yes, I was wondering if he was here. I had a terrible headache. But I'm okay now. It seems to be getting better. I'll just go and lie down."

"How did you get on today? Any news on the engines?"

The woman's gaze dropped. "No, I'm sorry. No news yet. They're rather complicated, you see, and I'm not sure yet what's wrong."

"I wanted to say, if you need any help...I sometimes tweaked the shuttle engines. I could lend a hand, if you tell me what to do."

MacAdam didn't seem to be paying much attention. She shifted her weight from foot to foot. "Thanks. So, I'll be getting along."

"Wait," said Carl, "don't you have to open the access hatch soon? Harrington said she'd be back around sunset. It must be getting on for that now."

"Oh yeah. Yeah. I just need to go get my tools."

"Right. I'll see you there."

14

Carl checked the time. He wanted to meet Harrington at the access hatch before taking her to speak to the mutineers in the brig, but he also wanted to check on Flux. He hadn't seen the little fella since he'd flown into the stasis room to warn him about the mutiny attempt. If he was quick, he could take a short diversion to his cabin.

Flux's favorite place in the world was Carl's bunk, where he would sleep under the covers with Carl, the sharp little talons at the ends of his wings scratching Carl and waking him. He sometimes wished Flux would sleep hanging upside down like the bats he resembled, but on the other hand, the fur on his belly was very soft and warm.

Carl pushed open his cabin door. There was no sign of Flux. His bedcovers had no familiar bump. Carl checked under them to make sure. The creature wasn't there. He opened his top cupboards nearest the air vent, but they contained no talking alien animals. He stood on a chair and stuck his head into the vent. He called his friend's name and waited.

The vents led throughout the ship and were very good echo chambers. Flux also had excellent hearing, far more sensitive than that of any human. If he was somewhere in the system and *wanted* to go to Carl—he had been known to sulk and refuse to come out on occasion—he would get to him within around five minutes. Carl waited a while and called again. Flux didn't appear.

He began to get worried. He couldn't find his friend, and he needed to get to the access hatch, right then. Why would Flux hide from him? He had nothing to sulk about, Carl didn't think. Had he been harmed during the attempted mutiny? He had to find the animal, but he didn't know where to look. Flux could be anywhere on the *Galathea*, including many places humans couldn't go.

Leaving his cabin, Carl wondered if he should ask if anyone had seen the animal. Flux wasn't supposed to be aboard ship, but since the crash, the rules and protocols seemed to be sliding. He could think of worse things than confessing he was harboring a stowaway, things such as never seeing his childhood friend again.

A woman approached, returning to her quarters with her food ration.

"Hey, I don't suppose you've seen a little flying creature around?" asked Carl. "He's about—" Carl was going to demonstrate Flux's size, when the woman interrupted.

"Your pet, you mean?"

Wide-eyed, Carl replied, "Well, he's not exactly a pet."

"No, sorry. I haven't seen him since yesterday. He's gone missing?"

"That's right."

"I'll ask around. Good luck finding him. Wouldn't like to lose the little scamp. He's a bit of a ship's mascot."

Carl watched the woman as she walked away. *A bit of a*

ship's mascot? It seemed that Flux had been getting around. So much for all his efforts to keep him a secret.

Word that Flux was missing spread quickly. The next two people Carl saw commiserated with him and said they would join in the search soon, and that there were others already searching. Though Carl was relieved that half the crew, it seemed, were looking for his lost friend, his anxiety continued to mount.

"Lingiari," a voice called.

Carl turned. One of the crew was some way behind him, beckoning.

When Carl hesitated, the man said, "We've found your pet. Come with me. I'll take you to him."

Carl jogged over and followed the man as he set off. "Where is he?"

"Flight deck."

"What's he doing there? Is he okay?"

"Yeah, yeah. He's fine."

Carl's pace slowed. If Flux was fine, why was he going to him, instead of the other way round? "How come he's on the bridge?"

The man glanced over his shoulder at the pilot. "He's, er, he's hurt himself. Just a little. Didn't want to worry you too much."

Slowing his run to a walk, Carl asked, "How'd he hurt himself?"

"It's his, er, wing. He flew into something."

Carl stopped. Flux had never flown into anything in his life. Except that one time he'd drunk a bit too much of Carl's beer. Something wasn't right.

Noticing Carl had stopped, the man called out, but not to Carl. "The pilot's here. This way."

It was a trap.

Carl started running in the opposite direction, but he wasn't quick enough.

Two explosions against his back were all he remembered before waking up. He was on the bridge. Haggardy's face was the first thing that swam into focus. How had he got out of the brig? The next thing he noticed was the trussed up form of his little friend. They really did have him. That part about getting Carl to go to the bridge had been true. Easier than searching the ship for him and running him down, he supposed. He wondered why Haggardy hadn't killed him. Yet, he mentally added.

"Pilot Lingiari, so glad to see you're awake. That was quite the massacre of the officers, wasn't it? You and Harrington should be congratulated."

Harrington. Was she aboard ship yet? Did Haggardy know when she was coming back?

"We didn't kill anyone," Carl said. "They died when the ship crashed. And it crashed because the master who you brown-nosed ordered Grantwise to land on the planet."

"Hmpf. Let's just say it was very convenient for you. I'll let Polestar and the Global Government decide the truth. For now, my confinement to the brig was unjustified, and it's fortunate for you that I was somewhat inadvertently released. As first mate, I am next in command, therefore the running of the *Galathea* is now down to me.

"However, I'm quite sure C.S.O. Harrington will hold a different opinion, and that's where you come in. It's clear you and she are close, and I'm sure it would pain her deeply to see you harmed. You, my lovely Australian flyboy, are my collateral. You'd better hope she accepts me as the rightful master of the ship. If she refuses, either you or your little friend here will persuade her with your suffering."

He turned to regard the strung up Flux.

"I don't mind which of you it is. I'll let you decide."

Flux cursed loud and long.

Haggardy's eyebrows rose. "Well, I've never heard such language from an alien before." He turned to the man who had tricked Carl into following him. "Put a gag on that filthy-mouthed beast, will you?"

15

J as didn't know how long the starship had lain there, or how it had arrived in its position deep underground. Built to withstand the rigors of space travel, something had worn it to pieces.

Weapon at the ready, she easily found access through its crumbling walls. Her mind whirled over the possibilities. Did the starship belong to the aliens who had infected the officers of the *Galathea*? Was it somewhere like this that Margret and the others had been when they'd become possessed?

It seemed unlikely. This place was rotten with decay. It reminded her of an ancient wasps' nest, the occupants long gone, and the narrow passages crumbling. She stepped over holes in the floor, placing her hands carefully against the soft walls for balance. She imagined the air smelled musty and close.

How could a starship end up so far underground? If it had crashed or flown directly into the planet's surface, Jas didn't think it would have gone so deep without entirely disintegrating, and there would be an impact crater. Or was it some kind of tunneling machine that had been abandoned there?

She went deeper into the ship, following the path secured by AX7 and AX12. They led her to a cylindrical room that had a ring of holes at eye level in the wall encircling it. Shining her headlight into a hole, the beams glinted on a material like glass at the end of a short tunnel. Beyond the glass was rock. She was looking out of one of the same kind of windows she'd seen from the outside. It definitely seemed like the ship had been intended originally for travelling through space. Or could it be a deep-water vessel? The planetary survey had revealed three deep oceans, but they were all far from where the *Galathea* had crashed.

Drawing back from the hole, she turned, and stopped. Her headlight had swept the center of the room and glanced upon something she hadn't noticed before—something different from the rest of the place. Something alive. Jas lowered her head to focus the light on the object.

Fleshy lumps were spread over the floor of the chamber, about as high as Jas's waist. They weren't old and decaying like the rest of the ship. They looked like some kind of fungus or inverted living bags.

Jas took a step toward the lumps. Immediately, joy overwhelmed her. She fell to her knees. Her heart lifted. She wept.

Through the excess of emotion, she tried to understand where the feeling was coming from, but mostly, she didn't care. She remained kneeling, unable to do anything within the grip of her feelings.

AX7 and AX12 remained motionless, awaiting her instruction, for a long time. Every so often, Jas would sob or gasp.

Some time later, the waves of raw feeling subsided a

little, and Jas broke away from their hold on her. She got up, finally registering the pain in her knees, and turned, puzzled, trying to understand what it was she was experiencing. What had happened immediately prior to the explosion of emotion? She had stepped toward the fleshy objects in the room's center. She swung around to them once more, lighting their smooth, satiny surfaces with her flashlight. Another surge of ecstatic happiness arose, and Jas fought to prevent herself from being overwhelmed by it.

It was those things. It had to be. Somehow, they were affecting her emotionally. Were they projecting their own feelings into her? If they had been alone down here while the ship had been decaying, it would be natural that they would feel joy at being finally found.

She turned on her mic to broadcast outside her helmet. "Hello?" she said. She took a step toward the lumps, but hesitated. Were these the aliens that had infected the crew? She knew she should get out of there, but she found she didn't want to. Something was telling her the aliens weren't harmful. She had to approach them, and it wasn't that she couldn't fight the compulsion, but that she didn't *want* to fight it.

Ripples of happiness coursed through her. In spite of herself, she grinned. The aliens seemed very pleased to have her attention, whatever they were. She gently prodded one with a gloved hand. A brief moment of fear sparked inside her, then pleasure.

In all her years in space, Jas had never encountered an alien so weird. How on Earth did they survive down there?

"What are you? How are you making me feel like this?" Jas didn't often pay much attention to her emotions. In fact, she would have described herself as pretty emotionless. These creatures were making her uncomfortable.

"AX7," she asked the unit, "do you notice anything different in your systems?" The defense units were intelligent in a sense, but they weren't supposed to feel any emotion, though she had never quite believed that.

"I notice no change in my systems, C.S.O. Harrington."

Jas was relieved. At least the defense units weren't vulnerable to these aliens.

She didn't know what to do next. She'd come here to find the aliens who had infected the crew, but instead she seemed to have found something entirely different. Were these fungi left behind by whatever had flown this starship? What should she do about them?

And should she continue the search for the hostile aliens? She'd been through the entire alien structure and found nothing. Nothing had approached her or tried to infect her, to her knowledge. She was none the wiser for her trip.

The joy the fungal bodies had somehow transmitted when they realized they'd been found indicated that they wanted to be rescued. Looking around her, it wasn't difficult to see why. If they remained there, the starship would eventually collapse and crush them. Also, these strange organisms might have benefits to offer. They'd survived all this time within the trap of the hostile aliens.

She couldn't decide what to do. To give herself time to think, she left the chamber to continue her search of the ship. In response to the sensations of despair that threatened to take over her, she turned to the creatures, and said, "I'll be back. I promise."

Commanding AX7 and AX12 to go first, she hadn't taken more than a few steps when the floor collapsed, already weakened by the heavy tread of the units. Jas tumbled down, hitting and then breaking through three floors in succession, until she struck hard metal. The surface was uneven, and her combat suit didn't completely protect her from the knobs and spikes that thrust into her back and thighs.

She was lying on top of a huge, complex machine. It looked like the starship's engine. She quickly checked her helmet display. No radiation. Unlike the rest of the ship, the engine looked comparatively untouched. Could MacAdam possibly use parts from this machine to fix their own engine? It seemed unlikely that the technology of different galactic species would be similar enough for that to work, but it was worth investigating.

It was time to get back to the *Galathea*. She had one, possibly two, important discoveries to report, and Lingiari had made her promise she would be back before sunset. She had been in the bowels of the alien structure too long.

By the time Jas had worked her way out of the starship and then up through the structure to the surface, she was bone weary. She gratefully strapped herself to the back of AX7 and told it to return to the ship. It was already dark, and brilliant stars were piercing the deep black sky. As AX7 jogged across the plain, she wondered what had been going on aboard ship while she'd been gone. She hoped MacAdam had made some headway with the engine schematics.

The access hatch was a dark hole in the side of the downed ship. MacAdam had opened it as instructed, and Lingiari must have kept it open, despite her lateness. She looked forward to seeing the pilot again. She would also go straight to see Lee. She'd been neglecting the navigator.

AX7 methodically climbed the side of the ship and swung up and through the hatch. As it entered the corridor, Jas unhitched herself from it and slid to the floor.

When she looked up, she found that her welcoming committee was somewhat different from what she'd anticipated. MacAdam was there, but there was no sign of Lingiari. In his place was the last person she'd expected—Haggardy, out of the brig.

Haggardy, free as a bird, standing right in front of her, an oily grin on his face.

"C.S.O. Harrington. How nice to see you again."

16

Jas was trapped. Sitting across from Haggardy in the mission room, next to MacAdam, she might as well have been as tied up as Lingiari. Haggardy not only had the pilot as hostage, but he could also command the defense units, and that meant he could do just about whatever he wanted. Maybe he already knew he didn't need Lingiari, and he was just having fun. Or maybe he knew that if it weren't for the fact that he might harm the pilot, she would be far more reckless about risking her life to go against him.

"So, Harrington, what's your assessment? You say there's a starship beneath the structure you visited, and that it's of alien make. Is it native to the planet?"

"I don't know. You tell me. Did you see anything like upturned bags when you supposedly managed to escape the alien infection that took the others?"

Haggardy's eyes narrowed. "I didn't."

"The creatures I found seem to be kind of telepathic, only with emotions, not thoughts. When I found them, they communicated that they were overjoyed, as if they'd been alone a very long time, or in fear of something, or both."

"A telepathic species?" He rubbed his chin. "Polestar might be very interested in those. Could be worth more than a penny. Did they seem dangerous?"

"Not at all. I touched one. It didn't respond, except emotionally."

Haggardy put his hands together, overlapping his fingers. "First things first, we need to get this ship space-borne. You've heard nothing from Earth?"

"No," replied Jas, "though we don't know whether it's because they haven't sent anything, or the comm hasn't picked up the packet."

"How far have you got with repairing the engines?" he asked MacAdam.

"Not far," the engineer replied. "I don't think I can fix them."

"Hmpf," said Haggardy. "Nothing from Earth, and we can't repair our engines. It looks as though this alien craft might be our best avenue for exploration at the moment. And I'm very curious about those creatures.

"Right. At first light, you and you," he pointed at Jas and MacAdam, "go back to that ship and see what you can find. Take portable scanners. And bring back those creatures. All of them if you can." He stood. "Meanwhile, I'm going to keep all my eggs in one basket. All three of you can spend the night here. The brig's occupied at the moment, with my rescuers." He gave a small smile, and after ordering defense units to bind Jas and MacAdam, he left.

〜

THE FOLLOWING DAY, Jas insisted that MacAdam cover herself up entirely before entering the alien structure with her. Lingiari had explained Lee's theory to them overnight, about how the structures might require a sample of their DNA to begin the infection process. Jas wished she'd had a combat suit to lend the engineer that would fit her stocky frame.

The woman had been mostly silent as they'd journeyed across the plain, and she remained taciturn as they made their way into the structure. Jas wasn't one for talking much, either, but she sensed there was more to MacAdam's behavior than her laconic personality.

"What do you think your chances are of finding something to fix the engines?" she asked her.

MacAdam snorted. "Honestly? Next to zero."

"Is that because it's alien technology? I suppose the two wouldn't marry well."

"It's not that," said MacAdam. "I looked at those engine plans all day yesterday. I read the manuals till my eyes were sore, but I'm not confident that I understand them. I'm sorry. I'm just not cut out for the job. I should never have taken it. It was just..." Her words faltered to silence.

"What?" Jas asked.

"Never mind."

"You need a good reason to work aboard a prospecting ship," said Jas. "Me, I had nothing to keep me on Earth. All the family I had, as far as I know, died on Mars. The colony domes exploded when I was a baby. My parents had just enough time to put me into a safety capsule. I was nearly dead when the rescuers found me. I don't even know who my parents were. The records were destroyed in the explosion. I could be one of several couples' child. No one knows."

"I'm sorry."

Jas shrugged. "I don't dwell on it. How about you? Why did you sign up?"

The engineer didn't answer for a moment, then she said, "If I tell you, do you promise not to laugh?"

"I promise."

"I...er...I signed up to get away from drink and drugs."

It was a struggle, but Jas managed to keep a straight face. "You thought you'd get away from addictive substances aboard a prospector?"

"I know," said MacAdam, shaking her head, "what was I thinking? Months of travel, confined to a starship with nothing to do but the same boring tasks over and over again. Not likely to find much drug abuse there."

Both women laughed. As their laughs faded, MacAdam said, more quietly, "I wanted to get my kids back. They got taken off me, you see, years ago."

"Now it's my turn to be sorry."

"No, don't feel sorry for me. I deserved it. They deserved better than me, rather. They deserved a chance at a good life. But I thought, I hoped, if I could get my life straight, maybe we could be a family again. But when I think about it, it's probably for the best that they don't see me. They'll be settled with new parents now, and they'll have forgotten about me. If I turn up to claim them, it'll only upset everyone. I should leave them be."

Jas wasn't sure that MacAdam was right. If the children were naturals, there were unlikely to be many couples interested in them. Nowadays, even couples who produced no sperm or eggs could have their own children and shape them to their desires. There were very few people who were altruistic enough to take on someone else's natural offspring, the result of a random genetic lottery with who knew what physical or mental problems waiting to emerge.

The two women followed the defense units down to the base of the structure. Jas led MacAdam into the cavern.

"Is that it?" asked the engineer as the side of the alien ship came into view.

"That's it. We can get in over there. But I warn you, when we approach the creatures I was telling you about, you'll probably feel overwhelmed with happiness for a while, until they get used to us and calm down a bit."

"Overwhelmed with happiness? I can deal with that. I haven't felt that way for a long time."

17

A block. It was a single, simple hexagonal block Toirien and Harrington had found next to the *Galathea* when they'd returned to the ship. No entrance or other break showed in its smooth gray surface. Harrington had paled at the sight of it, but she'd offered no comment. There seemed to be nothing for either of them to say. Whatever was living on the planet that had infected the officers, it seemed like they knew the ship was there, and they had plans for it. On the backs of the defense units, Toirien and Harrington had gone quickly into the ship and left it to the units to bring up the telepathic aliens. Toirien had secured the hatch tightly once everyone was inside.

Her experience of the telepathically relayed emotions of the aliens, which Harrington had unofficially named Paths, was such that it was like a run, and though the run was indeed high, coming down brought her lower than she'd ever been. She realized that the happiness they filled her with was almost entirely unfamiliar. Only dim, drug-hazed memories of the time she'd had her children with her came close, and since that time, her only moments of pleasure had been when she'd been able to escape the hard reality that was her lot in life.

After passing through the chamber that held the creatures, she'd descended with Harrington into the ship's engine. But the machinery made no sense to her, based on her understanding of the *Galathea's* engines. She couldn't find any similarities, nor recognize any parts, nor understand how the thing moved the ship through space.

After long hours of exploration and study, she'd silently shaken her head at Harrington. It was no use. Maybe if the chief engineer had survived, he might have made something of it, but understanding the technology was beyond her.

All that had been left for them to do was to transport the fleshy lumps back to the ship. They'd lifted from the floor like fungi pulled from soil, radiating waves of joy. It was impossible to explain why, but both she and Harrington had no doubt that these strange creatures were completely harmless, and they were ecstatic to be taken from the starship. They'd packed them onto trailers and the defense units had hauled them across the plain.

Back aboard the *Galathea*, after placing the aliens in quarantine, Toirien had persuaded First Mate Haggardy to allow her to return to her cabin. The man acquiesced, perhaps realizing she didn't pose him any threat. She had no interest in the running of the ship nor anything else.

Throughout the day, Toirien had been hoping for and anticipating the moment when she could get back to her cabin. When she arrived, it was with great relief that she saw no one had discovered the few drops of myth she'd secreted away along with the hypodermic needle and syringe she'd pilfered from the medical center.

The room was empty. Her bunkmates were away in the

canteen eating their evening rations. She needed to start her run immediately, before any of them came back.

She lay on her bunk and pulled down her pants. She tried to recall the place her supplier had shown her to inject the drug all those years ago. He'd told her the myth would work wherever it was injected, but for the maximum effect, you had to hit one of a few perfect spots. She craned her neck to look along the length of her bare midriff and thighs. It had been somewhere between her hip and pubic bone, she seemed to remember.

It was ironic, Toirien thought, that when she was at her lowest, she had the very thing that would take her the farthest she could get from her utter misery. She wondered whether, if it weren't for the promise of the ecstasy of myth, she wouldn't have unclipped herself from the unit that had carried her up the ship to ensure a quick, painless death on the ground below. Maybe, once this run was over, that would be an idea she would carry out. It would be quick at least. She didn't want to be around when whatever was in those blocks decided to come out and get them.

Holding the skin taut between the fingers of her left hand, she guided the needle home and depressed the plunger on the syringe. The second the myth hit her system, she was gone. The syringe slipped from her hand, the needle still in her flesh, and hung to one side. Toirien's respiration sped up, her mouth gaped, and her eyes were open but unseeing.

18

Jas was in the middle of a standoff with Haggardy on the bridge.

"What do you think we're going to do?" she exclaimed. "Leave the ship? You've got the defense units under your control. Do you think we'll round up the crew and persuade them to commit mutiny? They've already seen what happened to Karrev. It isn't like they're going to want to follow in his footsteps. And if *we* start anything, the units will put a stop to it easily enough. You let MacAdam go. Why not us?"

Haggardy regarded her from beneath his brows as she sat at his feet, her ankles bound and her hands tied behind her back. Jas still hadn't figured out if he'd been infected or not. She'd missed that first phase, when the victims showed that touch of inhumanity. Now, he seemed normal. If Haggardy was infected, she supposed he would have been leading them all into the nearest structure so they could be possessed too. He would be forcing them into that structure that had appeared beside the ship, yet he hadn't. That didn't make sense if he had been taken over by an alien, unless there was something preventing him from doing that, something she wasn't aware of, or that didn't fit in with his plans right then. Maybe the man in front of her really was all Haggardy and nothing else.

He leaned forward. "You never liked me, did you, Harrington? Well, I've got news for you. I never liked you either. Always doing everything by the book, getting in the way of common sense and everyone's chance at a bonus. Ms. High and Mighty, weren't you? You know, it wasn't just me, either. No one liked you."

"Oh, grow up, Haggardy. Doing your job isn't about being liked. Face it—you need us. You need Lingiari to fly the ship, and you need me to keep you safe and everyone else under control." Jas wasn't convinced about that last part herself, but she hoped she sounded convincing to him. She didn't relish the idea of another night on the hard floor of the bridge. The ship's temperature had equalized with the outside, and a chill had seeped into her bones.

"And keeping that animal tied up is totally ridiculous," Jas added. Flux's bindings and gag had been on him for more than twenty-four hours, and the creature looked ill.

Haggardy snorted and stood, but he was knocked to the floor. The ship rocked violently, as if there was an earthquake. The floor shook and seemed to drop several centimeters. Haggardy had lost his smug, haughty look, and he gripped the floor, terrified. Jas stared at Lingiari as she tried to figure out what was going on.

The movement stopped, and Jas went to speak, but before the words left her mouth the vibration started again. They weren't only shaking from side to side, they were lifting and then dropping to a lower level. They were sinking into the planet surface.

Her heart froze as she realized what it meant. That was

what had happened to the starship at the base of the structure. It had once been on the surface, but the ground had opened up and it had been drawn gradually deeper and deeper down into the soil and rock.

If they didn't get off the planet soon, the same thing would happen to them.

19

———

A vision played in Toirien's mind. She was traveling head first down a tunnel, carried on a breath of warm air toward a welcoming glow. She knew that everyone she'd ever loved, everything she'd ever wanted in life, lay at the end of that tunnel, bathed in the gentle light. Tears ran from her eyes and down her face, and they dripped from her chin before the balmy breeze lifted them and bore them away. She reached out with her arms, eagerly speeding herself on, anticipating the moment of arrival. The limbs she saw before her weren't her own. Her muscled, freckled forearms had been replaced with long, lithe, tapered specimens, just like the arms of someone modded for physical perfection.

She burst from the tunnel into the light, which was as warm and comforting as a mother's embrace. Joy suffused her being, and she floated, twisting and turning gently in the pure love that seemed to envelop her. Toirien spread herself wide, and her physical body and her mind melded with the glow, suffusing it so that neither were separate from the other.

As a part of this ethereal entity, she oozed herself wide, feeling with her senses the edges of her domain. But she was limitless. She encountered beings similar to herself. Others who were part of the one, unknowable, nameless whole. Toirien reached into the souls of these other beings and became one with them, perfectly harmonious and entire.

Immersed in the completeness, she became aware of others different from the rest. Snatches of thought and glimpses of shadows flitted through her perception, too fleeting to understand or behold. These beings left behind them jarring vibrations that upset the harmonious unity. As these shadows faded, other beings appeared at the edge of her consciousness—beings who seemed to see into the depths of her consciousness, and to the great, weeping wound at her core.

These beings approached and lifted her up, pulling the tendrils of her disintegrated self from the ether, and carried her away. Toirien fought. She rolled and jackknifed and tried to prevent herself from being taken from her bliss. She tried to scream, but she had no mouth and no vocal chords. She tried to hold onto something, but she had no hands and there was nothing to hold on to in that intangible, sublime place.

She struggled until she saw them. She knew who they were immediately. Their small, stocky figures, their bouncing ginger curls, their bright smiles. But as she drew nearer to her children, she realized this couldn't be them. They were too young. They would have grown in the inter-vening years since she'd last seen them. They couldn't be real, and yet they seemed more real than anything she'd ever known.

The glow faded. Her feet—all of a sudden she had feet

—hit pavement, and she was running, running into the arms of her darlings. Wrapped around each other, Toirien couldn't breathe in enough of her children's sweet scent, feel enough of their enveloping arms, bury enough of her face in their soft hair.

"Mammy, Mammy, you came back. We knew you would come back one day. And you're here. We missed you so much. Now you'll never, ever leave us again, Mammy, will you? We love you, Mammy, we love you."

Toirien wanted to say, no, that she would never, ever leave them again, but somehow she knew the words were wrong. Her children were wrong. Something stopped her from giving into the vision that was playing out before her.

"I can't," she said. "I can't. I can't come back to you. I'm too far away. There's too much space between us, and too much time has passed."

"Yes, you can, Mammy. You can come back. There's nothing wrong. Nothing wrong at all. Silly Mammy. All this time you've been worrying—worrying about nothing. Things aren't as bad as you think. You only need to try."

Toirien's heart raced. She stared into the face of little Grace, trying to reconcile her childish features with the words that were coming out of her mouth.

"Silly Mammy," echoed Joan. "Come back to us. We've been waiting for you a very long time. Don't make us wait any longer."

The little girls broke their embrace with her and held hands with each other. "Bye-bye for now, Mammy. See you soon." They skipped away.

The image of her children was replaced by the view of her bunk screen and the ceiling of her cabin. Toirien's run had ended, and she was suddenly completely sober. A soreness emanated from her hip. She looked down to see the hypodermic needle hanging from her skin. Wincing, she drew it out. A drop of blood welled up.

Her cabin mates hadn't returned, which meant she'd only been gone a short while. The run should have lasted hours. She couldn't understand it. Toirien pulled up her pants and fastened them. Her heart was racing, and she breathed heavily, though she didn't know if these were the effects of the myth or her strange vision.

She could hardly believe what her children had said in her dream. It was all impossible. Yet what they'd said was true. She hadn't believed the evidence of her eyes. She'd always thought she would mess up again, and that she would let everyone down. She'd never believed the fix could be such a simple, easy thing. She hadn't trusted in herself, but had always focused on the worst possible outcome.

Maybe her dream was just the meanderings of her drugged imagination, but even if there was the slightest chance they weren't, if she'd been taken to a place where she could connect with her children and the truth of what they'd said, it was worth telling the others. It was worth trying. What did she have left to lose?

She had a weird feeling that she'd been strongly shaken while she was out. As she swung her legs over her bunk and jumped down, another vibration started up.

20

Toirien pushed open the door to the bridge and staggered as she burst into the room. The ship was shaking again.

"I thought of something," she shouted over the grinding noise. Haggardy, Harrington and Lingiari were all staring at her after her sudden entrance. "I should have said it before, but...I...I couldn't find any damage to the engines when I scanned them. I thought I just didn't understand what I was looking at. But I've just realized...we haven't even tried to start the engines since we crashed. What if they aren't that badly damaged? What if they just shut down because of the crash-landing? We could try to start them up and see what happens."

"Is this correct?" Haggardy asked Jas and Lingiari, raising his voice. "You didn't even *try* to lift off the planet?"

The vibrations stopped. Jas and Lingiari were staring at each other.

"I never thought..." said Lingiari. "The crash was so bad, I just assumed..."

"Me too," said Jas. "We never thought to even try it. To

think we might have been sitting here all this time when we didn't need to..."

"Let me try," said the pilot, trying to get to his feet. "Untie me, Haggardy."

The first mate considered a moment, then instructed a defense unit to release Lingiari from his bonds. He slid into the pilot's seat, brushed the screen in front of him with his fingertips, and flipped some switches, but the screen remained dark. He turned to MacAdam. "It was worth a try, but she's dead. Not a squeak from her."

"The systems are dead," said Jas. "Doesn't mean the engines are."

"Same thing," replied Lingiari. "It's not like I can crank her to start her up. Sorry, it's a waste of time." He unclipped his harness and stood up.

"We've got to try again," said Jas. "This vibrating—I think it's the planet drawing us in, like it did with the other starship. Maybe it does that with every ship that lands on it."

"Krat," said Lingiari. "That makes sense."

Haggardy collapsed into the master's seat and ran a hand over his face.

"Wait. Maybe it's just a power thing," said Toirien. "The ship's been on emergency power since we crashed. Maybe there isn't enough power to get the system working."

Haggardy looked up. "It's worth a try." He spoke to Toirien. "You, connect all the defense units to the ship's system and direct all their power to the pilot controls."

"No," said Jas. "Not all the units. We need some to keep Lee in stasis."

"Hmpf," said Haggardy, "I saw you've been using defense unit power to maintain our dearly departed navigator. Well, her prolonged departure has finished. *All* available power, do you understand?" he said to MacAdam. "Can you do that?"

The engineer hesitated.

"No," exclaimed Jas and Lingiari. The pilot flew at Haggardy, but he fell before taking more than a few steps, stunned by a defense unit.

"You can't kill her," shouted Jas, her hands clenched into fists. "She...she's your best asset. I've never known anyone so smart. What if your plan doesn't work and the engines won't start? What are you going to do then? We're going to be dragged down into the planet, and Lee might be the only one who can figure out what to do. You *need* her."

The terrible grinding vibration started up again. The unconscious Lingiari flopped to and fro. Haggardy and MacAdam grabbed whatever they could to stay on their feet.

Haggardy said to the engineer," All the units except those powering the stasis room." He added, looking at Jas, "For now." MacAdam left the room, taking Haggardy's defense unit guards with her. But the man also had a gun, which he trained on Jas.

She nearly wept with relief at saving Lee. She also despaired. She'd never realized how dumb and ruthless Haggardy was. He really would have killed Lee. With him running the show, they'd all be lucky to survive.

After a short time, MacAdam returned. Lingiari turned, groaning, onto his back as she entered the bridge. "I've attached all the units to the pilot control system, except the ones powering the stasis room. We can try again."

Rubbing his chest where the stun beam had struck, Lingiari returned to the pilot seat. He tried the controls once more. The others watched and waited. He shook his head. "Nothing. She's dead."

"Perhaps we need a little more power," said Haggardy. "I

appreciate your attachment to your shipmate, Harrington and Lingiari, but honestly, she's dead meat. It's time for a noble sacrifice to save the crew. *You'll* appreciate the sentiment, Harrington, I'm sure."

"You misborn fool," said Jas, pushing herself awkwardly to her feet. She teetered, her ankles bound, her feet pressed together. "I keep telling you that woman is the best asset this ship has. If you turn off her stasis, we're *all* dead meat."

"Hmpf. Well, let's see if you're right, shall we?" He instructed MacAdam to untie Jas's bonds. "Let's go and speak to Navigator Lee. We can explain the situation, and let her plead for her life."

Blood slowly returning to her feet, Jas wobbled as she followed the first mate to the stasis room. Lingiari and MacAdam came along with them. On the way, the ship experienced another bout of violent vibration. Jas wondered how far they'd sunk into the ground. If the engines really had been undamaged before, were they the same now?

Lee seemed unchanged when they pulled her container out from the wall. Sparks fastened the electrodes to her scalp. Jas's heart was in her throat. It would be unspeakably cruel to wake the navigator up only for her to find out she might be about to die, along with the rest of them.

"Who's there?" Lee asked.

"It's me, Sayen," said Lingiari. "Harrington's here, too, and the engineer, MacAdam—"

"And I," said Haggardy. "How nice to speak to you again, Navigator Lee."

"Haggardy?"

"That's Acting Master Haggardy to you."

Lingiari said, "Sayen, we need your help." He explained MacAdam's theory about the engines, and the fact that maybe they couldn't start them because the ship was on emergency power.

"Wait a minute," said Lee, "the ship's systems would have shut down during the crash. Didn't you try to reboot?"

"We didn't," exclaimed Jas. "We didn't even try to restart them. I don't believe it."

"That's what happens when you have a security officer and a pilot in charge of a starship," said Haggardy, acidly. " Well done, Navigator Lee. You may have just saved your life."

CARL HAD WARNED THE CREW. Everyone was in their crash seats. Haggardy had taken the master's chair, and even Flux had been unbound and was sitting in a bag that Carl had strapped into a seat on the bridge. The little fella's head peeked out, and his long, black-tufted ears were switching to and fro. He seemed to have got a lot better as soon as he was released.

Haggardy had insisted that Harrington stay within his sight. She was sitting at the comm control.

Carl's pilot's screen was live, the measurements and graphs glowing as bright as they ever had, which was a welcome sight after days of darkness. Lee's advice had been spot on. The ship's systems had rebooted like a dream. The interior lights had come on, the air circulation system had whirred to life—everything had started up as if it had never stopped. Cheers from the crew had echoed down the corridors.

Haggardy's patience had been tested by MacAdam's insistence that she check and doubly secure the hatch she'd opened. She'd also made the access hatches to the engine airtight. Though the engine could operate perfectly within the vacuum of space, the crew could not, and she didn't know if the hull had been breached during the crash-landing.

Now, the most important thing was to get off the planet.

"All clear," Carl said into his mic. "Lift off in one minute." He would use the RaptorXs to fly them into orbit. It would take a huge amount of fuel to push the massive starship into space, but they had no choice.

A ping sounded from the comm desk.

"It's a packet," exclaimed Harrington. "Polestar's sent a reply to Lee's message."

"Read it out," said Haggardy.

"Packet from Navigator Lee aboard the *Galathea* acknowledged. Please proceed to K. 23198f, otherwise called Dawn, where you will receive further instructions from the resident authorities."

"They don't want us to return to Earth?" asked Carl.

"Doesn't look like it," replied Harrington. "I guess they don't know whether or not we're carrying infected crew."

"So what're they going to do with us at the new planet?" asked Carl.

"We will comply with the directive from Polestar," said Haggardy.

Carl's screen was flashing. "Prepare for lift-off."

The RaptorX engines fired, and Carl's chest constricted. In front of him, the visual of the planet shook before dropping slowly down. Whoops and hollers could be heard from the rest of the ship.

"You beaut," exclaimed Carl. Exhilaration flooded him as the *Galathea* lifted from the frigid, barren plain below and moved slowly toward the horizon, which began to bend into a curve as they flew higher. He'd completed this maneuver once before, just once, and that had been in a simulator.

Both the ship and his nerve were holding up, however. Carl lifted the ship steadily through the atmosphere as it gradually thinned and the sky darkened. Acceleration pressure pushed him into his seat. The first stars became visible, twinkling in the thin gas of the upper atmosphere.

After what seemed like a long time, they achieved orbit, and Carl cut the Raptors. He floated briefly against his seat harness until the *Galathea's* artificial gravity kicked in.

He'd done it. He'd lifted a starship off from a planet, and maybe it had been the first time anyone had done it. He'd never heard of another pilot landing—okay, crashing—a starship onto a planet and taking off again. He might be the first.

"Lingiari," said Harrington, "I've sent over the coordinates in that packet. Do you want to input them? We're going to try to starjump, right?"

Oh yeah. He'd forgotten about that for a moment. Carl shelved his satisfaction for later contemplation.

He had a ship to fly.

JAS'S STORY CONTINUES IN
DAWN

SHADOWS OF THE VOID BOOK 3

Sign up to my reader group for a free copy of *Starbound*, the Shadows of the Void prequel that tells the story of what happened to Jas Harrington in Antarctica, for discounts on new releases, review crew invitations and other interesting stuff:

https://jjgreenauthor.com/free-books/

The Books of Shadows of the Void - Complete Series

Prequel: Starbound
Book 1: Generation
Book 2: Stranded
Book 3: Dawn
Book 4: Shadowrise
Book 5: Underworld
Book 6: Burned
Book 7: Trapped

Book 8: Mars Born
Book 9: Shadow Battle
Book 10: Shadow War
Books 1 - 3 The Galathea Chronicles
Books 4 - 7 The Earth Chronicles
Books 8 - 10 The Galactic Chronicles

Copyright © 2021 by J.J. Green

All rights reserved.

No part of this book may be reproduced in any form or by any electronic
or mechanical means, including information storage and retrieval systems,
without written permission from the author, except for the use of brief
quotations in a book review.

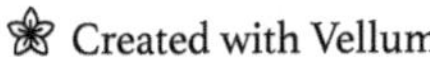 Created with Vellum